A Minor Inn-Convenience

Oaklawn Coffee Book 2

Emmie J Holland

ISBN: 979-8-9863115-7-9

EDITOR: Kenna Karlsson (Instagram: @kennakarlssonwrites)

COVER ARTIST: Meghan Lee (Instagram: @wolfefantasy)

Contents

To the girls who boycott millennial gray in their design choices.
You're saving the world one home project at a time.

Trigger Warnings and Sensitivity Reading

Dear Reader,

It is my desire to ensure that everyone who picks up this book feels comfortable in doing so. Because of this, I have provided a list of trigger warnings. Be kind to yourselves.

Explicit Sexual Scenes

Swearing

Challenging Family Dynamics

Dear Reader,

As I dove into Noah and Lennon's story, I knew I would need to hire a sensitivity reader for this particular book.

Noah's mother is Vietnamese, and his father is white. He is written and depicted in art as such.

Since I am a white writer, I knew it would be important to self-reflect, research, and take other important steps before publishing this novel. This story has been combed through by a paid sensitivity reader for anything that may perpetuate harmful stereotypes. However, if you read this and find that something doesn't sit right with you, please don't hesitate to reach out to me via email.

esteinbrauthor@gmail.com

Oaklawn Coffee

A Minor Inn-Convenience is the second novel in a series of interconnected standalone books. These books are best experienced in order, but reading out of order will not negatively impact your reading experience as each book stands on its own.

The complete series is listed in order below:

A Bucket List Birthday Griffin & Ellis

A Minor Inn-Convenience Noah & Lennon

A Bittersweet Summer Wes & Cass

One

Lennon

I'm staring at the listing again.

As I click around on my laptop, waiting for the realtor to arrive, I'm sucked right back into the first time I toured the old house.

White paint peeling off every railing, a wrap-around porch that could kill you, and squirrels living in the attic. It was perfect. It *is* perfect. And while the price tag still makes me want to respond to the very fake Instagram message offering to be my sugar daddy, I wouldn't have it any other way.

This place is my dream.

I can see right through all the house's faults and imagine it as the perfect bed-and-breakfast—the business I'm about to call my own.

The glass door to the coffee shop opens, pulling me out of my thoughts. A cool breeze whips through the tables, rustling papers on a table near the front. That autumn air mingles with the scent of espresso and chai, causing me to breathe a little deeper—to feel more relaxed.

That is until I look up.

That deep breath leaves me in an irritated exhale as soon as I see him.

Dark hair styled perfectly atop his head, eyes framed by a pair of glasses, and an irritatingly put-together outfit that screams *I am an English professor.*

Because he is.

But does he need to advertise it so plainly?

Noah Ashwood, my best friend's boyfriend's best friend, strides toward the counter and offers the barista a devastating smile. And if the description of how I know Noah isn't irritating enough, then the front-row seat to the petite blonde eating up every ounce of charm the guy exudes is.

It's like his charming demeanor follows him in a thick cloud.

Something akin to a cloud of foul body odor.

If Ellis, my best friend who unintentionally connected me with this fuckface, was here in the same situation, she would ignore him. It's wise to ignore the man who single-handedly ruined the best date you've ever been on for literally no reason aside from his own pride.

It's the smart thing to do.

The mature thing to do.

As Noah grabs his cup and turns on his heel, making to walk directly past my table, I remind myself that ignoring Noah Ashwood is the noble thing.

Yet–

"What an unpleasant surprise." I roll my eyes, returning my gaze to the laptop in front of me, clicking randomly on the screen to look busy and indifferent. With how low the brightness is on my laptop, I'm met with the vague outline of my green eyes, appropriately pissed off, the red hair tumbling down my shoulder in a singular braid, and the freckles smattered across my face.

My mother used to call my freckles *cute*.

It's unfortunate because I'm trying to exude anger and judgment. Not *cute*.

Squinting against the low brightness of my computer, I try to gaze upon the images of the house again. The much younger version of myself would be proud to see every detail carved into the wooden banister–the original hardwood floors that hold history–*stories*. When I toured the house, I asked as many questions as possible. I wanted to know about the families that had lived there–very obviously giant families because six bedrooms happens to be excessive. It's as if the walls held onto those stories and were vibrating with the need to release them and put them out in the open.

Or maybe that was a structural issue I ignored. I can't be sure.

Unfortunately, the realtor hadn't known much about the home's history, but seeing as I'm meeting him any minute, the chance that he learned something is high.

I'm also itching for an opportunity to share my excitement about my new purchase. It's not like I can call home. My father had always hoped I'd choose a different route–something unrelated to hospitality. With my older sister's success as a doctor, I seem to be the family disappointment. We must be related because we both love taking care of people. I just don't want the stakes to be as high as death.

Looking at the listing, my pride swells. It's a badge of honor–a feeling I'm trying like hell to preserve. However, that pride is dimmed by the presence of one very haughty English professor.

"Well, if it isn't the fire-breathing dragon herself." Noah offers a wide smile when I give up and glance in direction, his dark eyebrow cocked as he grips his giant coffee in one hand. Somehow, the insult sounds like flirting when it rolls off his tongue.

I hate it. And honestly, who needs a coffee that large, anyway?

I blink at him, casting judgment over every inch of his tall frame. Noah's not as tall as his friend Griffin. Maybe six-foot? I'm hoping my gaze makes him feel a solid five-foot-three. Just shorter than I am, so he knows I think he's wretched.

"Careful," I say, leaning back casually in my chair. "I bite."

"Sounds enticing."

All I feel is hot disgust. It sits in the pit of my stomach like a heavy weight, holding me to my chair and preventing me from standing and throwing a punch at his perfect fucking face.

"That's disgusting."

Noah chuckles before taking a sip of his drink. "What are you doing here, Lennon?"

"Meeting someone," I supply, watching as the wheels turn in his brain. I wonder if he's thinking about ruining another date.

About five months ago, Ellis had an art show, and I, like any normal human being, brought a date I'd met on one of those weird dating apps. Everything was going well until Noah jumped in–making asshole comments and practically growling at the man like a feral dog.

At least, that's what it felt like. I'd only caught Noah's hateful glances during introductions and the tail end of their argument on the patio just before everything imploded.

My date left early.

Then he ghosted.

And now I fantasize about digging a massive hole in my backyard, throwing Noah's body into it, and leaving him to die.

"Who's the lucky guy?" Noah asks, and it's so casually friendly I almost feel bad for plotting his murder.

Almost.

I sigh, tapping my screen again and staring at the massive white house I'm about to purchase. I can't lie to the guy. Lying makes me uncomfortable—makes my skin itch. "My realtor," I answer before glancing up at the door one last time–hoping that said realtor will save me from this unpleasant conversation. "I bought an old house just outside of the city." My face scrunches. "Well, I am about to buy the house. Thus, the waiting on the realtor thing."

"New place to live?" he asks, and my eyes snap to his.

"I'm converting it into a bed-and-breakfast. It's been my life-long dream to convert an old house into a space where I can lure innocents and breathe my fire at them." The way my excitement leaks out–the sheer desire to have someone, *anyone,* acknowledge my accomplishment brings an uncomfortable wash of shame. It just screams *daddy issues,* and for that, I hate myself. I try to hide my weakness by raising a brow in challenge–daring him to diminish my success.

He lifts a shoulder, seemingly unaware. "Makes sense."

There's an uncomfortable silence, one that rings in my ears and makes my head hurt. I'm still waiting for him to jump into some well-thought-out thesis about why owning a bed-and-breakfast is the worst kind of business. I'm waiting for him to tell me I'm not cut out for hospitality and encourage me to use my business degree on something far more logical, like a well-paying office job.

It's what my father would say.

My sister, too.

Fuck.

Instead, Noah just looks at me, and something pained flickers in his brown gaze, causing me to wince. I can't handle pity. If he sees through my charade, I will insult him into oblivion and ponder going to therapy for my shit coping skills.

"Listen," he starts, the vulnerability in his voice making it clear that whatever he is about to say might not be about me at all.

Oh god, I cannot have this kind of serious conversation in this coffee shop. How does one comfort a grown man? Will he expect me to pat his back? Wipe his tears?

"About the art show."

Relief floods through me at the fact that he isn't about to cry in my lap or some weird shit. Annoyance is the next emotion to take center stage, and that bitch is a whore for attention whenever I'm around *Professor* Ashwood. I hold up my hand.

"I'm going to stop you right there, Ricky Bobby. Slow down because I don't want to talk about the art show. You were, and still are an asshole. I'd like you to leave me alone. You're lucky you got this much conversation out of me at all."

Noah winces. "Ouch."

The espresso machine sounds again from behind the counter, murmuring swirling in the coffee shop from the people who surround us–completely oblivious to everything that just happened. Outside, everything I love about early autumn happens to be repressed by the weird Midwestern heat that happens to linger this time of year–sticking around like an unwanted pest.

Sort of like Noah.

Something about the English Professor needles me and puts me off balance. It could be the way he always appears so polished–like a pillar of perfection. He walks around with an air of success and accomplishment with his fancy clothes and his fancy job. Meanwhile, I'm sitting here trying like hell to convince myself and my family I'm just like that.

Put together. Successful. Unbothered. Confident.

The man picks at every insecurity I try so hard to hide.

Clearing my throat, I shift uncomfortably. Lucky for me, I see Peter walk through the door, a wad of papers in his hands as he makes a B-line for my table.

Saved by the realtor, I guess.

"Lennon," Peter's deep voice cuts in before Noah can formulate a response. "So glad to see you. Are you ready to get this done?"

"Beyond," I answer before my eyes cut to Noah. "My acquaintance was just leaving."

Peter looks visibly uncomfortable, but I don't care.

Not when Noah nods once, mutters a few parting words, and strides out the door of the coffee shop.

My eyes linger on his back when he goes, and I make a note to text Ellis and tell her we are never coming to the coffee shop on Oaklawn again. I don't care that she likes the homemade pop-tarts. We simply cannot risk running into Professor Ashwood.

Peter clears his throat, sitting across from me at the table, and I push the distraction from my mind.

At least–

I don't think of Noah until after I sign the mountain of initial paperwork.

Unfortunately, once I leave, the dumbass finds his way into the forefront of my brain, and I quickly divert the thoughts into something more murderous.

It's far safer than remembering how his ass looked in his trousers.

Two

Noah

If there's anything I know about Lennon, it's that I know absolutely nothing about her at all.

My job requires that I be the one who knows everything, so my inability to figure her out remains a constant issue. It's bordering on obsession, and for some fucking reason, she seems to be *everywhere* since Griffin and Ellis got together.

Nothing about her makes sense. For starters, she's the one who struck up the conversation to begin with, so having her dismiss me the way she did seems like I was set up to be humiliated.

I'm not usually this unlikable. Why the fuck does she find me so unlikable?

I feel like one of those people trying to reach her about her car's extended warranty, but Griffin refuses to give me her number. I'm pretty sure he's afraid of her, which is completely understandable.

Lennon is confident, assertive, and borderline abusive.

It's kind of hot.

But mostly off-limits.

The glass slams behind me as I find my way onto the sidewalk in front of the coffee shop. Warm autumn air fills my lungs as I look up to see shades of red, gold, and orange decorating the surrounding trees. Fall's peak hasn't quite reached Ohio yet, but the colors promise it will be soon. Even if the temperature is just a shade too warm. After that, we enter the utter despair that is stick season–mud, empty branches, and gloomy gray skies.

I check my watch, realizing I'll most likely be late for my own office hours. Sitting in my small office at the college and waiting for students begging for my help is not my favorite part of the whole English Professor thing, but it's a necessary evil.

I wince, knowing exactly how many emails will fill up my inbox before I arrive.

I'm not positive physical letters won't also start flying from beneath my door like an ignored acceptance letter to Hogwarts.

Finding my way to the car, I pull out my keys, unlock the door, and slide in. After placing my coffee in the cup holder, I grab my phone out of my pocket. For what feels like the millionth time since last spring, I look at the read and unacknowledged Facebook message I sent–the one I had to get shitfaced to even think about passing along. To make matters worse, Alexis didn't even have the dignity to respond.

I don't blame her, though.

She probably thought I was lying in some last-ditch effort to ruin her marriage and get her back. Again, something that wouldn't make sense to begin with because I was the one to break off our engagement, and it's been five years. The ship has sailed.

Maybe that's why I felt the need to send her the message after I saw her husband show up at the art show with Lennon four months ago. It could have been the guilt of leaving her, or maybe a small part of me felt like karma was finally finding her. Either way, the message sits untouched–my explanation to Lennon still pending.

I close out of the app and call Griffin. He picks up on the second ring.

"Noah?"

"I need Lennon's number." I push the key into the ignition, turning it until the car rumbles to life.

"Dude, when are you going to stop asking?" I can hear the thread of laughter in his voice. "Ellis said Lennon doesn't want you to have it, and I'm not going to go behind her back. Lennon's her friend, not mine."

Ellis and Griffin started dating almost nine months ago. It was just a few months before Griffin quit his job working at the college where I teach and go on tour with his audio engineering abilities. Somehow, his traveling hasn't stopped them from moving forward at full speed.

Griffin was never one for casual relationships. I'm positive he doesn't approve of my lifestyle choices in that department, either. Casual happens to be my defining characteristic. It's far easier to keep a careful distance in relationships, though I'm not sure *relationships* would be the right word. I fuck. I have straight forward conversations about expectations and tread carefully so as to not create or experience feelings of disappointment.

I'm *good* at casual. Very good.

Griffin, on the other hand, reeks of devotion and commitment. And in this one particular instance, it's pissing me off.

"It's important," I say, flicking on my left turn signal.

"You can't sleep with Lennon, Noah."

I blink that idea away before turning on the speakerphone and setting my device in the one free cupholder next to my coffee. I really need to figure out the Bluetooth situation, but I've been too busy to bother. And somehow, I always seem to forget when I'm not actually in my car.

"Is that what you think?" I finally answer, somewhat offended, not really surprised. "I'm trying to apologize about last spring. Trust me, sleeping with Lennon is the furthest thing from my mind."

Mostly.

I can't say I haven't considered it. We've spent enough time in each other's orbit that it's crossed my mind. There's no denying Lennon is attractive, but something tells me the woman doesn't do casual. For as biting as her temperament can be, I've seen her loyalty, too.

She's fiercely loyal to her friends. Sex is probably no different, and I can't afford to get tangled in that kind of web. Too many mutual connections. Too complicated.

"Just apologize in person the next time we all hang out. Simple, and not sure why you haven't already."

I huff out a breath. "Not simple. It's more complicated than that."

"How so?"

I don't know how to tell him I confronted her date on the patio at the art show while she was off somewhere else. There are too many moving pieces. Explaining that I had once been engaged to a woman named Alexis, had been cheated on, broke off the engagement, watched on social media as she got married to some stranger who had slept in our bed, and then saw said stranger show up with Lennon on his arm seems like too much. It's one giant confession, and I still haven't even figured out how to explain it all to Lennon. I'm not even sure I want to. I guess I'm banking on "he's a mutual friend of mine, and he's married."

"It's–" I pause, my mind cycling through all the details. "Complicated."

"Sure is. Look, I got to go. But the answer is still no. Maybe find another way if it's so important?"

Of course.

After hanging up the phone, I focus on the drive and try not to spiral. I find my way to my office, sit my ass down, and wait for the next student with enough balls to beg for a better grade.

I would obviously give them a better grade. I'm not some scary monster, and taking initiative is a trait that deserves reward.

Sipping my coffee, I scroll through my email and note that I was, in fact, correct. I have at least four saying they had waited past the start of office hours but never saw me.

Perfect.

The day rolls on, and somewhere between my visits, I find myself with some downtime I shamefully spend scrolling through Instagram. I'm thoroughly distracted, and Lennon must have me blocked. I know she has the app, but I can never find her. I'm also certain that I'm not so old I couldn't figure it out.

I'm just clicking around when I find an interesting account that follows Ellis—somewhat suspicious. It says something about inn adventures in the bio, and the profile picture looks a lot like Lennon.

Upon further investigation, I ascertain that this account most definitely belongs to Lennon. I'd recognize the red hair and freckles anywhere. Her little bed-and-breakfast dream has been years in the making because the page reads like a blog, detailing her time saving up to open her own inn and showing pictures of the ones she's visited. There, at the top and according to the caption, is the picture of her new house.

Every post boasts of rich stories and the enjoyment of *people*. It's so contrary to the Lennon I know, the person who pointedly hates humans. Or maybe she just hates me.

Quick-witted and devoted to details, every post points out architectural details from various time periods. She seems to enjoy keeping the integrity of a space and honoring the lives of the people who previously occupied the homes.

My brows raise, and I take another sip of coffee, now cold, before clicking on the message icon. I tap out an explanation, knowing for damn sure I'm about to end up in the message requests section, along with every fake account ever.

But beggars can't be choosers, and I'm tired of the whole charade. I can't spend the rest of my life worried and obsessing over the girl who strikes up a conversation just to call me an *acquaintance* in front of her realtor.

· · ● ●·● ● ·· ·

A soft, feminine voice sounds from the door to my office, dragging my attention away from my computer. "Excuse me, but I'm actually looking for room 112, and I can't seem to find it."

I look up, trying to reorient myself after nearly five pages of what might be the worst rhetorical analysis essay I've ever read. Honestly, the paper acts as either a cry for help or a student's confession of a long night binge drinking at some college party.

Auburn hair, full red lips, and a black skirt that hugs every curve.

Fuck me.

I'm in for a pleasant distraction.

"Dr. Neilson," I greet, a smirk pulling at the corner of my mouth.

Her wide smile sends a buzz through me, and I close my laptop. I haven't seen Julia Neilson since last semester, something she does twice a year to speak in Dr. Anna Martin's class. I've never listened to the presentation, nor have I asked about it. Anna and Julia are friends, and Julia and I–

Well, we're familiar.

"Sure seems like you've found the right place," I say, allowing my gaze to linger briefly on those lips before checking my watch. They're the same lips that, just last spring, had been wrapped around my–

Shit.

5:45, and I have a class in fifteen minutes.

Julia's eyes narrow, but a small smile remains. "Thought I'd set up early," she says, arching a brow. "Figured I'd stop in to say hello. I haven't talked to you since last spring."

"Right." I push the sleeves of my sweater up to my elbows, stretching out in the office chair and placing my hands on the back of my head. The room feels ten degrees hotter, my memories playing like a movie as I take in her every curve.

Just something casual, she'd said, and that's the exact definition of our relationship.

Casual. Uncomplicated. Unattached.

Julia hums, her eyes flicking over the bookshelf in the corner, and I stiffen.

Textbooks and some of my favorite works of literary fiction decorate the shelves–completely disorganized. It's a direct contrast to the rest of my orderly office. Most of the books on that shelf mean something to me. I'm more attached.

I find disorganization provides a better representation of my life. Polished on the outside, but internally, I'm a mess.

The fear of being perceived suddenly makes my chest hurt, and I desperately wish she'd stop looking at the shelves. I've slept with Julia enough times to be cautious. Our entanglements need to be categorized in a very specific way–nothing too vulnerable.

"Got any plans tonight?" I ask, knowing full well she will understand what I'm implying. It's a routine now. I know nothing about the woman aside from how she looks naked, and by the way she looks away from the shelves, I'm reminded that she feels the same.

It's the perfect arrangement.

"I was actually hoping to make some plans for after my presentation."

Her cheeks blush, and the shade of pink blends in with the freckles on her nose. Something about the freckles–the way she tilts her head to the side in consideration. It's right, but feels so wrong.

Earlier today, I could have sworn I saw Lennon's cheeks flush while she kept her eyes trained on her laptop. For the briefest moment, I thought maybe she'd been embarrassed, but her biting remarks following proved that to be incorrect.

Julia, in contrast, is softer–giving. The flush of pink on her cheeks gives away every thought–every feeling. She's easy to read and asks for what she wants.

I don't think Lennon asks for anything. She would be the type to demand it.

My blood heats, and I'm not sure who is causing it.

"I'd be up for making plans," I finally answer, realizing just how much I need a distraction. Anything to get my mind off of Lennon, desperate apologies, and the whole host of pictures I spent a good thirty minutes scrolling through.

I hope I didn't accidentally double-tap the photo she posted from spring break two years ago. She'd been sunbathing by the pool at a small bed-and-breakfast in Put-in-Bay.

That image needs to be replaced.

I stand, grabbing my laptop and my satchel, and knowing that I need to get to my own evening class. "What do you think about eight-thirty? I can meet you back here."

Julia licks her bottom lip before a smile stretches across her face. "Depends. What did you have in mind?" She pauses, her eyes flicking down in a very obvious show of what she's thinking. It seems we are on the same page there.

I allow a knowing smile to work at the corners of my lips. "I think I could come up with a few ideas."

"Eight-thirty, then."

And with that, she turns, striding down the hallway and leaving me alone with my thoughts.

There are about a million and one things I'd like to do with that woman, but somehow, I don't think any of them will live up to the fantasy now running on repeat in the back of my mind. It's unwanted.

It's not like I would ever consider touching Lennon. Something about it feels off–wrong? Maybe it's that I would be hooking up with someone too close to the friend group. I can't see a world in which *hooking up* with her would be a good thing.

Still, it doesn't hurt to imagine it a little.

The memory of Lennon's voice echoes in my mind as I rush to class.

I bite.

I fucking wish she would.

Three

Lennon

"I need Noah's number."

It's a shameful declaration, but alas, we are here.

After receiving a brief message on my second Instagram last week, the one where I forgot to block him, I decided that I probably need more information. I've got a plethora of questions for Noah Ashwood–questions he will answer as penance.

For starters, *what the fuck?*

And also, *are you actually fucking kidding me right now?*

"Oh, how the turns have tabled," Ellis says, tapping a finger on the bathroom vanity.

I stand up, looking into the back of the toilet like I have any idea how to fix this thing. The guy on YouTube was very convincing when he explained what my problem was and why it wouldn't flush, but for some reason, nothing is working.

I turn to Ellis. The smirk on her face looks like she knows something even though there's nothing to know.

My face scrunches as I pull my phone out of the back pocket of my jeans, click on my contacts list, and get ready to add one very annoying professor to the list of people I don't want to talk to. "He tried to reach me through my Instagram. You know, the one where I have documented this whole process."

With brows raised, Ellis picks her own phone up off the counter. "Really went the extra mile, did he?"

"He's persistent. I'm not entirely convinced he isn't from Utah and on a very particular kind of mission."

A text pops up on my screen: Noah's contact information. Despite my stubborn attempt at staying far, far away from the man, I add him to the phone and shoot off a text message—risking a Mormon conversion.

> **Me:** First of all. What the fuck, Noah?

I hope I was clear enough because, honestly, Noah wasn't clear at all. I've been looking at the message nonstop, wondering what possessed him to send *he was married and on a date with you* out of nowhere. And to follow that very short message with *you deserve better, Lennon.*

Stupid.

Ellis leans over to look inside the toilet, where a small amount of toilet paper floats in the bowl. *Thank God I didn't take a shit in the thing before discovering it didn't work.*

"Any ideas on how to fix it?" I ask. "YouTube University is failing me right now."

I blow out a breath, and Ellis scrunches her nose. "I could call Griffin and ask, but I'm at a loss here. It's getting late, and I need to go, but I'll ask him."

"It's not even six o'clock." I close the lid to the toilet and sit down, my hair flying in all directions as it attempts to escape the bun atop my head. It looks exactly how I feel with this damn house. *Maybe I was in over my head.*

No.

I can't think like that. If I think like that, Dad wins.

"I have to babysit Eloise for B, so six is, in reality, very late." Ellis types something out on her phone before shoving it in her pocket. Eloise happens to be Ellis's niece–the little girl she babysits constantly. After the death of her mother, Beatrice took Ellis in as her own. Being so young, the woman didn't get married until Ellis was older and properly positioned as full-time babysitter.

It's not malicious–just frustrating.

"I guess it *is* late if you have an entire babysitting gig. Don't you work tomorrow?" I turn to face her, noting the tension through her shoulders. Ellis has always had trouble saying *no*–something I make up for in strides.

"Well, yeah," she starts. "B was kind of in a pinch. She's dropping Ellie off at my house."

I look to the toilet–a lost cause. "Tell her I can do it," I say.

"What?"

"I'll watch Eloise here. There's a working toilet upstairs, so that's a nonissue. You can take the night to have a loving phone conversation with your sometimes long-distance boyfriend who is touring the state with that weird indie band." A small smile tugs at my mouth when I see the tension slowly leech from her body. "You are all welcome at my house. Anytime. Eloise is no different."

"Yeah, yeah." Ellis waves a hand. "I'm welcome as long as I fix something." She smiles, and I know I've got her.

I nod. "Exactly."

Grabbing her phone again, Ellis types out another message while muttering a soft, *are you sure.*

After a generous amount of reassurance, she grabs her things from the very empty dining room and heads out for the night, letting me know B will be by in about an hour.

She will probably snuggle Griffin's cat, Simon, make a snack, and have the best evening of her life.

I, on the other hand, sit in the bathroom with a broken toilet, waiting for my five-year-old supervisor to arrive and save me from boredom. That is until I receive one very confused text message from the last person I want to be talking to.

Noah: Who is this?

Classic

> **Me:** It's Lennon, you asswipe.

I hit send before setting my phone down and standing to wash my hands in the sink. At least the faucet works.

The house was destined to be a fixer-upper. I'd saved enough for a down payment and renovations, but the budget is tight. Especially with all the debt I'm acquiring to turn this place into my dream business. I can feel the stress tightening my shoulders already.

My phone vibrates on the counter.

> **Noah:** You text exactly as I thought you would.

> **Me:** What is that supposed to mean?

> **Noah:** Just as brutal on the phone as you are in person.

> **Noah:** What's up?

He has to be kidding. This is one sick joke. Does the man not remember sending me a message where he stated that the man I went on a date with months ago was actually *married*? It's kind of hard to forget and is obviously the only reason I am texting him after months of refusing to cough up my number.

If he's going to pretend the message doesn't exist, then so will I. Lure him into a false sense of security by striking up a friendly conversation. Then, and only then, will I force him to confront what he professed.

While I'm still pissed off at him, it doesn't stop my curiosity or my desire for more details. At the very least, Noah is pleasant to look at. At the very most, he's fun to insult.

It could be fun.

I snap a picture of the broken toilet, the lid to the back still missing. After sending the photo, I type out an accompanying message.

> **Me:** Trying to fix this

His response is almost instant.

> **Noah:** Do you even know how to fix a toilet?

> **Me:** YouTube is a very useful resource.

> **Noah:** I'm glad

> **Me:** It's not working though. Might need to pay a plumber.

> **Noah:** Hopes and dreams not all they cracked up to be?

I roll my eyes, the smile still forcing its way to my lips. I must be one lonely bitch.

Or maybe I'm just ovulating and thus remembering the way Noah looked in the coffee shop as he strolled away.

> **Me:** There has been a bit of a struggle.

> **Noah:** Want some help? I might be able to fix it.

Staring at the message, I think, very briefly, that it would be beneficial if I thought through my decisions more. Ellis is cautious and tends to err on the side of *safe*. I do whatever feels right. I guess I'm just following the vibes.

And right now, the vibes of saving a few hundred bucks sound super appealing.

Plus, he's nice to look at, and I'm enjoying this conversation.

> **Me:** For free?

His next text takes longer to come through and gets me worrying that *help* might not actually exist out there.

We are all in this alone. I don't care what Zac Efron says.

> **Noah:** Not free. I'll fix your toilet if you talk to me.

Pressing my lips together, I stare at the screen. This is it. He's addressing his insane Instagram message.

> **Me:** Is this about what you said on Instagram last week?

> **Noah:** I'm assuming that's what your opening text was about.

> **Noah:** And yes. It's about that.

So, he is not an idiot, then.

I weigh my options. One conversation with a hell of a view for a working toilet? Seems like a deal to me.

> **Me:** Fine. But only if you fix my damn toilet.

Noah: So demanding.

Me: This is a business arrangement, Professor Ashwood. I'm a paying customer. I just so happen to be paying with my time.

Noah: Point taken. Send me your address.

I wince, quickly typing in Ellis's number and regretting it the moment I hit send. It's not like I thought the entire thing through. Volunteering to babysit immediately before inviting a strange man to the house to fix my toilet?

"Hello?" Ellis answers, clearly confused as to why I'd be calling her so soon after her departure.

"Do you think B will mind if Noah is here fixing this toilet while I watch her kid?" I ask. "I swear it's not weird. He offered to help, and he owes me. Plus, Eloise would be a great buffer. I can protect her from harm. She can protect me from exchanging my granola aesthetic for something more akin to dark academia. I wouldn't be good with trousers, Ellis." I place the phone between my shoulder and my ear before walking to the kitchen and gathering supplies for peanut butter cookies. I'm sure Beatrice will appreciate sedation via sugar. "Can you even imagine me in a pantsuit?" I add.

"Noah?" Ellis questions. "Why would Noah be coming over to fix your toilet?" She sighs. "You know what, I don't even want to know, Lennon. Let me text her since I just pulled into my driveway, though I'm sure she won't mind. It's not like she hasn't met the guy. He practically lives with Griffin when he's home."

There's a brief pause, the annoying sound of tapping, and then she's back. "Yeah, so it's fine. For whatever reason, my aunt trusts you."

I smile, pulling the phone away from my ear and touching the speaker icon. "She has great taste. Besides, I'd throw myself on a fire before I let any harm come to that little squirt." I type out my address, feeling satisfied.

"Hey," Ellis starts. "Thanks," she says, sincerity laced in the word. "You're actually doing me a huge favor."

"I took some time off to deal with the house. It's really not a big deal, and you know I only pretend to hate children."

Ellis snorts. "Don't make it weird, though. Things are weird between you two. Don't you dare make it weird on little Ellie."

"You got it, Captain." I press my tongue into the side of my cheek, staring at my phone in the hopes that another text will come through from Noah. My stomach flutters with nerves, and I'm suddenly aware of my body betraying me.

The last time I saw Noah, I'd still been mad at him. I'm not saying that his very vague justification for doing what he did absolves him from any wrongdoing. I am, however, acknowledging that if he knows how to fix a toilet, I would hear him out. Some of my anger might fizzle away with that grand gesture.

My pocketbook will thank him.

"Love you, Lennon."

I smile. "That's gross."

When I hang up, I get a text from B that she's on her way with Ellie, and the spike of nerves eases. With Eloise running around the house, I will have the perfect excuse to ignore Noah should things be anything but completely normal.

Maybe the presence of a small child will push him into a sincere apology–soften him.

After all, he ruined my date. He should beg for my forgiveness.

I'd like to see him beg for forgiveness.

I pocket my phone and grab a glass from the cabinet. With that very unhinged and intrusive thought, I can't help but wonder if letting Noah Ashwood into my home will become some sort of grave mistake.

Four

Noah

I don't think I've ever dressed myself faster.

I'm not sure what lit the fire under my ass, but getting her address seems like winning the jackpot with the way she's kept me at a distance all this time.

The opportunity to explain myself happens to motivate me, but the acceptance into her space sends a thrill through my blood. It's a stamp of approval I've been desperate for since last spring.

At the art show, Lennon had found her way to the patio to see her date pissed off and walking out with a shitty *it's been fun*.

I'd been caught red-handed, and I guess she needed someone to throw her anger at. That person being me, obviously.

Months of disapproval, snide remarks, and unfortunate misunderstandings, and I finally have an opportunity to set the record straight and crack the code that is Lennon Yarrow. While I feel a bit like Sam from *Holes*, fixing her toilet for such an opportunity seems like an adequate exchange.

Charlie walks back into her bedroom, still very much naked, with her blonde hair kissing her shoulders. Her eyes meet mine as I pull on my other shoe.

"Sorry," I say, but the word sounds hollow. "Something came up."

I stand, my body itching to leave.

A soft hand slides over my shoulders, down my chest as she rises onto her toes, her lips ghosting over my ear. "Why don't you stay this time?"

Oof. That is my cue to exit the premises and note that this will not be happening again.

I met Charlie at a bar just inside the city. It's one Griffin, Ryan, and I frequent. One drink buys you access to all the arcade games, so it makes for a good time.

The night Charlie had invited me home, she'd been trying her hand at Pac-Man, and I'd been trying my hand at getting to know her better. And by that, I mean learning the sounds she made with me inside her.

Since Alexis, I've played this part numerous times. No attachments and casual sex satiates whatever desire I used to have for a relationship. The sex is great—better than it was with my ex, which probably says something about that relationship to begin with. But I spend most of my days with my family or working at the college. The sex offers an opportunity to get all my pent-up energy out of my system—an escape.

It's a fantastic arrangement that requires no strings, no commitment, and no opportunities to give away any pieces of myself aside from what my physical body can offer for a short time.

The relationship aspect is a sensitive topic, but essentially, it's way easier when the sex remains casual.

Which is why this will be the third and final time I will have slept with this woman.

"You know," I say, gently grabbing her wrists. I kiss her palm to ease whatever guilt I feel. "I think maybe this should be the last time we do this."

A frown pulls at the corners of her lips, still swollen. "You don't mean that."

I wince. "I thought I was pretty clear about what I wanted when we started this."

Charlie turns, grabbing her t-shirt from the floor and pulling it over her head—her movements rushed. The band shirt hits mid-thigh, and while normally the sight would send me in for another round, I can't stop thinking about the goddamn toilet I need to fix. I'm not handy, I don't know exactly how I'm going to pull this off, but I *need* to talk to Lennon.

"You said we were welcome to sleep with other people and that things would be casual," she says, rehashing what I'd told her from the very beginning.

"Exactly."

"Noah." Her head tilts to the side, shoulders slumping. "This is like the fourth time we've slept together in the last two months."

"Third," I correct, running my hand through my already mussed hair. I hope Lennon doesn't see it for what it is–sex hair. Oddly enough, I don't want her knowing how I spent my evening.

Charlie huffs, crossing her arms in front of her chest. "Okay, third." She tucks a strand of hair behind her ear as her body language shifts. "So, we've slept together three times. I originally thought it would be just once, but then you texted me, and we saw a movie."

I can see her closing in on herself, and I feel it–the itchy guilt that makes me want to crawl out of my skin. It's not like I wasn't clear with her, but I hate feeling like she misunderstood my intentions.

There just can't be a relationship. Charlie doesn't know me, and I don't know her. There is also the very real possibility that if she were allowed to get to know me, I would not be what she was looking for.

I'm good at what I'm good at. And at this point in my life, it's teaching literature and sex.

Not at the same time.

The emotional cost of a relationship is far too high.

"I know." I inhale the lingering scent of lemongrass from the candle on her dresser, releasing the breath with an exasperated sigh. "But I still said no strings attached."

Charlie's eyes refuse to meet mine as she stares at the wall, her arms still crossed. "I haven't slept with anyone else." Her voice sounds small.

Yikes.

My brain short circuits. I'm at a loss here.

"I never said we had to be exclusive. Again, you were welcome to sleep with other people." The words cut cold, their bitter taste souring any feelings of attachment Charlie might have been harboring.

This was probably a mistake.

"I just thought–"

I clear my throat, and her words die out. Her brown eyes look lighter–almost hazel–and I'm pretty sure she's about to cry.

Shit. Shit. Shit.

"You know what?" Charlie waves a hand. "Don't worry about it." She walks back toward the restroom, refusing to look at me. "Have a nice night, Noah."

Standing in the center of her bedroom, it takes me a moment before my feet are moving. I'm no stranger to situations like this, but it doesn't change the fact that I feel like an ass.

And maybe I am.

I can't offer what Charlie is looking for. Relationships require too much trust and vulnerability, and I'm not sure I could offer those things again. I'm not cut out for that kind of commitment.

Eventually, whatever novelty there is will wear off, and Charlie will find herself looking for fulfillment elsewhere.

It's exactly what Alexis did.

The disappointment that flooded Charlie's features follows me onto her porch and all the way to my car sitting in her driveway. I can't say that the guilt doesn't sting.

Or maybe the stinging was the brisk autumn air that appeared as the sun descended on the horizon.

When I enter the address for Lennon's new house, I leave the guilt and discomfort behind me. My fingers tap against the steering wheel, desperate to get rid of my anxious energy as I listen to the YouTube tutorial I found before pulling out of Charlie's driveway. Hopefully, by the time I get to the house, I'll be able to fix the toilet, no problem.

As for Lennon's distaste for me? I'm not sure that's something that could ever be fixed.

And I'm not sure why I'm so obsessed with wanting it to be.

Five

Lennon

When the sound of gravel and the flash of headlights force me to look up from the puzzle sprawled across my living room floor, I make my way to the large window and watch Noah get out of his car.

"Who's that?" Eloise asks from her spot on the ground. "Also, this puzzle has too many pieces."

"Just someone who is going to fix the toilet, and I think it's time we make some cookies anyway."

Ellie pops up, knocking over the box on her way to join me by the window. She presses her nose to the glass, and we watch together as Noah strides to the door.

He's dressed professionally–as always–looking like a dark academia wet dream. It's insulting how he just walks around in trousers and a sweater, his sleeves rolled up to his elbows and exposing toned forearms. Honestly, I'm trying like hell to find something–anything to dampen his appeal. The black hair styled lazily in combination with the *glasses*? God, do I have a glasses fetish?

While I'm a little more curious about Noah Ashwood, considering he walks around looking like *that*, it still doesn't change the fact that he ruined my date–no matter the reasoning. I'm set on digging my heels in and hating him a while longer.

When he knocks on the door, I turn to Ellie. "Why don't you head to the kitchen? There's a stool in the pantry, and we are going to need that." I tap my chin, ignoring the second knock on the door. "Oh! We will also need the eggs. Do you think you can be super careful? It's a big job."

"Auntie Lennon, I'm almost six. I can carry eggs." Rolling her eyes, Ellie skips down the hallway, leaving me to answer the door.

The brisk air floats in with the scent of his cologne. He smells like tobacco leaf and vanilla with a mix of rum. It's exactly what you'd expect an English professor to smell like.

He fits the part. That's for sure.

"Hey," I say, my tone dead and my face flat. "Toilet first. I'm babysitting."

His eyes widen. "Babysitting?" he questions.

"Ellis deserved a night off. Her aunt needed some help." I shrug. "Eloise isn't so bad. I kind of like her."

"Auntie Lennon!" Eloise yells my name from the kitchen. "I just didn't crack *any* eggs. I told you! I told you I can carry eggs."

Noah fights off a grin, holding the strap of his leather bag. "Auntie Lennon."

"It's not the first time I've helped out." I point at him–glaring. "Toilet."

"Of course." He strides around me–giving me another long drag of whatever intoxicating scent he's wearing.

I absolutely *must* be ovulating. This is an insult to women.

"Where's the bathroom?" His eyes scan the entire entryway, dress shoes scratching across the rustic wooden floors, before his eyes catch on the incomplete puzzle sprawled all over the hardwood in the next room over.

I shut the door behind me, rushing past him and leading him to the half-bath tucked in the hallway on the way to the kitchen, and as expected, little feet sprint toward me, Ellie's grin contagious as she practically vibrates with excitement.

"Do you have any apples?" she asks.

I don't look back at Noah, though Ellie glances his direction–just briefly. "Apples?" I question.

She stands on her toes, pointing to a tooth and wiggling it dramatically. "Mommy said when she was little, she lost her first tooth because of an apple."

"And?" I tilt my head, encouraging her to continue.

She points harder at her mouth. "See! I have a tooth to get rid of."

Noah clears his throat. "You could always tie a string to it. Tie the other end to a door and slam it shut. That thing will come right out."

Ellie looks horrified, and I toss a glare over my shoulder. "What is wrong with you?"

"You're just the toilet guy," Ellie asserts, crossing her arms, and I've never felt more pride save for the moment I bought this house.

"Yeah, Noah. You're just the toilet guy."

I send her back into the kitchen, turning to show *Mr. Toilet Guy* exactly where he will be working for the better part of the evening.

Rude? Maybe.

But the idea of calling a plumber gives me a visceral reaction.

"There it is." I point to the toilet, my tools still sprawled across the tiled floor. "Just one of many renovations I'll be working on over the next few months."

Noah drops his bag just outside the door before standing next to me and making me realize just how small this bathroom is. The urge to get away is strong.

I can't be this close to him while under the influence of whatever cologne he has. "Fixed a lot of toilets in your day, Professor Ashwood?"

Noah smiles again, and for what it's worth, his movements seem confident as he bends down to assess the damage. *How tall is he again?* He pulls on the handle, and absolutely nothing happens.

His lack of response is unsettling. "What did you think? I lied? I told you it doesn't work."

"I've never fixed a toilet," he admits, and I blink, wondering if I heard him right.

"Then why are you here?"

Grabbing his phone out of his pocket, he unlocks it just to pull up the same fucking video I had been watching earlier.

Irritation zaps the horniness right out of me. I'm cured. "Fucking fantastic."

"Should you be cursing while babysitting?" he questions.

"Should you be telling small children to yank their teeth from their mouths with string and slamming doors?" I bite back.

Noah shakes it off, standing and wiping his hands on his trousers. "To answer your question," he begins, our height difference now way too apparent. It sends a little buzz through my body. *Goddamn it.* "I'm here to talk to a pretty girl, of course."

I frown, and if a frown could be loud, mine sure as hell is. This cannot be happening. He probably wants in my pants, and I have a five-year-old in the kitchen getting into who knows the fuck what.

So, while I may also want that, I'm busy, and I've heard too many things about Professor Ashwood to allow something so disastrous to occur.

"You're supposed to be here to fix a toilet," I say, reminding myself that based on all descriptions of Noah's extracurricular activities, he's probably a petri dish for every STD on the market currently.

"I'm figuring that part out," he responds.

I scoff, squeezing past him and making my way to the door, waving a hand.

"I already feel bamboozled." And I certainly cannot stay in the same room as him. "I'll leave you to it. Come find me when you're done. We will be in the kitchen. Baking peanut butter cookies."

I scramble away to find Ellie sitting on the counter, an open jar of peanut butter in her lap and a spoon caught in a death grip as she confidently eats from the jar.

"Well," I start, gently taking the spoon from her hand. "This jar of peanut butter is now yours."

"Does that mean I get to keep all of the cookies?"

I smile. "Oh, absolutely. I wouldn't dare offer these cookies to anyone else. They're for you and you alone, my dear."

She's beaming, and I refrain from explaining that she just contaminated the entire batch by double dipping and claiming the peanut butter all to herself. I'm sure her aunt won't mind. I'll just send the batch home.

My mind drifts to the very real presence of a man in the other room, and I try to stay focused on my task–give the child overwhelming amounts of sugar and games–save Ellis from another late night before work.

It all proves near impossible with Noah under my possibly leaky roof. I'm just stressed. Old houses, brisk autumns, and shitty heating are getting to my brain and my ovaries.

· · · ● · ● ● · · ·

"It flushes."

I look up from where I sit on the couch, feet propped on an ottoman, giving me some distance from Noah. Ellie crashed after way too many cookies and a helping of chocolate milk before B stopped by to pick her up.

Needless to say, Noah's toilet repair skills could use some work. If I were paying him by the hour, I'd believe he were intentionally screwing me over.

Not so. He just sucks at home repairs, but the toilet flushes, so I refuse to complain.

Thank fuck.

Neglecting to set my e-reader aside, I look back at the text on the screen. The male main character just called the female main character *prissy*, and somehow, someway, it read like a compliment. A very hot compliment.

Noah shifts his weight to the other foot, wringing his hands briefly before clearing his throat. "You said we could talk."

I glance up. "Isn't that what we are doing?"

Do I want more information about the cursed patio argument and the ruined romance I was living out in real time? Yes.

But what I want more is for Noah to work for it.

What *it* is, I don't have the slightest clue.

Without another word, Noah drags himself from where he stood to the spot right next to me on the couch. The brown leather creaks when he leans back and props his feet up, making himself comfortable.

He glances at my book.

"What are you reading?"

I quickly press the lock button and throw the thing to the side as if that will save me. "You poke your nose in my love life, and now you're out here sticking it in my hobbies? Could you be any worse?"

I swear he winces before a smile replaces the expression.

"I just want to know what you read for fun. If I were to guess, I'd bet on something violent. You don't come across as one of your standard *Pride and Prejudice* women."

I turn my nose up at him. "So what if I am?"

Noah raises his eyebrows. "I would be very surprised."

"I'm full of surprises."

Our faces are close—so close I can see the small lines at the corners of his eyes when his smile widens. I also watch them smooth out with that same smile drops from his lips. The soft lights of my new living room highlight the golden undertones of his skin. I can't help staring at him. Noah Ashwood is objectively beautiful.

It's ridiculous.

"You owe me an apology," I say, hoping my tone sounds clipped.

"I do." His words melt over me like warm caramel.

God. I need to get away from him.

Closing my eyes, I lean my head on the back of the couch, trying to retreat without making it obvious. I wince. "How did you know he was married?"

"Lennon." I can hear the sympathy in his tone, and I don't dare open my eyes. "It's complicated. I know his wife."

My brows furrow. I've heard plenty of stories about Noah, most of them through Ellis. I know how he spends his free time, and I know he is the direct inverse of Griffin.

The man can commit to nobody.

Realization dawns on me, and hot fury works its way up my throat. "Oh my God." I finally open my eyes. I can't believe I sat on this very couch convincing myself that Professor Ashwood could be anything more than an absolute rake.

I thought that learning to fix my toilet meant something. That an apology could mean something. I thought—

I stand up, placing the ottoman between us. "You slept with his wife, didn't you?"

Noah chuckles, and I don't know how he can remain so calm. "Technically, yes."

Disgust burns like the fiery pits of hell.

"For fuck's sake, do you have *any* morals at all? Here I thought you were coming to help me out as a way to make amends." I'm pacing. It's the only way to ease the anger.

"I was engaged to her, first," he admits, and the room goes quiet—my thoughts right along with it.

I stop pacing, turning to face him fully with my hands on my hips. The entire conversation is giving me whiplash. "I beg your finest pardon? What is this? An episode of Jerry Springer?"

Noah runs his fingers through his already mussed hair. He's no longer smiling, and I get the sense that I've made him uncomfortable. "I don't really talk about this."

I scoff. "You literally showed up here *to* talk."

"Fine. Yes. You're right." He gestures for me to sit back down, but I can't bring myself to move. Not until I have answers.

"While I was finishing up my doctorate, I was engaged for a brief time." He looks embarrassed, and something about that tugs at whatever sympathy I can give. "I'd dated a girl, Alexis, all through high school. Close to graduation, my last one, I'd found a wallet on our nightstand."

Shit. This is *not* the story I was expecting.

"Checked the driver's license, and it did not belong to me or my fiancee. Long story short, they got married a year later. So, a little over three years ago."

Oh my God. She cheated on him, and I went on a date with her now husband. I suppose karma has a way of making its rounds. "Ouch," I say.

His dark eyes meet mine. "Yeah, ouch." It almost seems like he wants to say more, but he doesn't, and I'd hate to press for too much.

His confession explains his willingness to chase off my date last spring. In fact, Noah Ashwood was actually saving me from myself.

I still can't help but wonder why he did it. It seems like this *Alexis* was getting what she deserved. No need to spare me. It was a first date. A damn good one, but that is neither here nor there. Especially now.

I wasn't exactly emotionally attached to the guy.

"It would be rude of me to ask more questions, but I'm kind of wondering what the other details are here," I lift a brow in challenge, and for what it's worth, Noah doesn't balk.

"Anxious to know more about me?" The corner of his mouth ticks up. "That'll cost you," he says, and his expression settles something in me.

I can only do so much serious conversation.

My eyes land on the cold fireplace across the room. It'll make for a great addition to this front seating area in the wintertime. Hell, it would be great to have it up and running now, and I wonder if Professor Ashwood is as good at chasing bats as he is at fixing toilets.

I turn back to Noah. "You could fix my fireplace in exchange for another conversation. Hasn't been usable in a while."

He chuckles, and the sound burrows beneath my skin and makes its home there. "That sounds like you might be getting the better deal."

Without warning, my lips tug up at one corner. "Maybe."

"I'd love to fix your fireplace, Lennon." He stands, rounding the ottoman until he stands directly in front of me, his gaze warm and inviting. "When would be a good time?"

That buzzing sensation returns, and I can't keep my eyes off his mouth as I replay the way my name rolled off his tongue. "You're going to actually fix it?" I ask. There has to be some kind of catch here.

Maybe Noah really wants in my pants. If not, this is incredibly odd behavior.

He may have just confessed some emotional trauma from his past, but the way he's looking at me—

"Sure," he says. The word rests between us, and it feels like an invitation. I can't think with him this close to me–can't think when he stares at me with his dark brown eyes or when he shows up out of nowhere fixing things and asking to talk to me.

The house is quiet as Noah remains motionless, neither of us moving, and I'm fully aware of how close we are standing. His eyes briefly flick to my mouth, and while the man seems to have some red flags–his promiscuity, his traumatic past, his lack of denim when it comes to pant choices–I can't help but think red flags have all sorts of uses. For instance, they can mark holes in a round of putt-putt.

I *do* love putt-putt.

Damn. What has gotten into me?

"Make out with me." The words leave my lips faster than my mind can keep up.

Noah's eyes widen.

Awe shit. Shit. *Shit.*

"What?"

This train is quickly derailing, but I started it, and I'm willing to follow it all the way down. "I said make out with me."

Noah swallows, his gaze resting on my bottom lip like he wants to drink it. Or maybe not, because the next word out of his mouth has embarrassment warming my cheeks.

"No," he says.

I lift my chin, trying to hide my discomfort. "Why not?"

He blinks, looking almost as if he's in pain. "For starters, weren't you just babysitting a child?"

"She's not here. I spent the better half of an hour making up stories about the house, then B picked her up. I figured you'd heard, but apparently not. So–"

He shakes his head. "I can't. I just–"

I'm being rejected by a man who sleeps around more than a cat next to a window on a sunny day. This is quite literally the worst moment of my life.

"I can't make out with you, Lennon."

I'm certain I didn't read him wrong. All the signs were there.

Weren't they?

"Okay," I say in response.

I turn on my heel, exiting the living room and plowing my way through the house to the bathroom. I will just make sure the toilet works and then dismiss him.

My mind is racing. I asked him after he confessed to me that he was *engaged* and she *cheated*. Could I be more of an asshole?

Normally, being an ass wouldn't bother me. I've accepted my personality and all its faults. I've accepted the fact that I absolutely do not think before I speak, and that's just how things go, but regret winds its way around my throat–making it tight.

My eyes sting, and I am thankful I hear his footsteps stop in the hallway. Thank fuck he didn't follow me into this bathroom.

"I'll be back tomorrow to check out the fireplace," he says just before the front door clicks shut.

I take deep breaths, digging my nails into my palms. There is no way that man will be over again tomorrow, that's for damn certain.

Six

Noah

Staring at the ceiling fan in the darkness of my bedroom, my thoughts race.

The house Lennon bought has a lot of potential. And while I know nothing about running a business or fixing half of the shit that's gone wrong there, I have no doubts that she'll be successful. She doesn't seem like the type to take no for an answer.

Except for tonight.

I knew the girl had been picked up. I was just looking for an excuse. Making out with Lennon after everything that happened would have been idiotic–reckless.

In the bathroom, I'd heard her giggling with the girl on the steps. Eloise, was it? They'd finished baking their cookies–the ones I did *not* get to try. Lennon had woven a tale about the fairy who lived beneath the steps, hidden away from the world. That is until a little girl who used to live in the house bribed the fairy with peanut butter cookies for a chance to meet the fairy.

Eloise had been enraptured–deciding to save some of the cookies for the fairy.

I'm fairly certain the story had been in an effort to keep the girl from eating too many cookies, and something about the way it was done, the way Lennon had made the world so magical, tugged at something within me.

I'd once thought my life would look like that–telling stories to children on the steps of a house I owned, and that wasn't what I wanted anymore.

Plus, it was weird–seeing Lennon in that light. I couldn't make out with a woman who so clearly has relationship potential.

Driven, confident, a homeowner, enjoys children.

I'd ruin that woman.

But as the ceiling fan continues spinning above me, all I can think about is the way the air thickened between us–the soft curve of her mouth. When her green eyes flicked down, that need wound tighter.

Loose strands of hair kissed the sides of her freckled cheeks. Everything I could have needed to entertain myself for the night was within my grasp, and when she asked me to kiss her–no–make out with her, I knew exactly what I wanted.

It took everything in my power to force the word *no* from my lips.

I've spent years saying yes—to women, to distraction, to momentary escape.

I couldn't say yes to her.

The complications that would arise from getting involved with Lennon were too numerous to count. *Are* too numerous.

For starters, there are the mutual friends, the memory of Charlie's look of disappointment tonight. I couldn't do that. Not to Lennon. I barely know her, but something about her makes it seem *wrong*. It could be how our lives are now tangled. As long as Ellis and Griffin stay together, Lennon and I are connected.

There's no way in hell I would have kissed her despite desperately wanting to.

Fuck.

The light from the clock flickers in my peripherals. It's way too fucking late for me to still be thinking about touching her. And yet-

All my mind can seem to conjure is the image of Lennon sprawled beneath me—red hair fanning out over my pillow as I sink myself into her.

She'd probably insult me while we did it—tell me I was terrible in bed despite the little sounds sneaking past her plump and parted lips.

I can't touch her—not really. I *won't* touch her, but after scrolling through the numbers in my phone, trying to think of anyone I could find to relieve this ache, I'm at a loss.

My hand slips beneath the waistband of my joggers as the image plays out in my mind. Wrapping my fingers around my hardened flesh, I move—stroking—pressing—sliding my hand in time with the imaginary thrusts.

Fuck.

Her body would be pliant—lips soft as she worked her way down my neck—my chest. If I got lucky, she might go lower—wrapping her mouth around where I needed her most and gazing up at me with that judgmental fucking stare.

My breath comes out in harsh pants as I pick up the pace, still imagining Lennon's full lips, thinking about the way she'd pop off the tip, sliding her body forward until I was nestled at her entrance.

When I picture her sinking down on my cock, my entire body tenses, my hand working in rhythm with the fantasy.

"*Fuck.*" The word is whispered into the dark as I feel the tension in my body release, the orgasm crashing through me like a fucking freight train.

I suck in a lungful of air and try to recover—center myself.

The worst thing I can do is imagine what it would be like to taste the one woman I can't be with. The worst thing I can do is lay in my fucking room as a grown-ass man and picture her while I stroke myself to completion. The worst thing I can do is show up at her stupid house to fix a fireplace when I have no knowledge of how to even go about that.

Spending time with Lennon is dangerous. That's for sure.

After cleaning up, I grab my phone, unable to stop myself—like she's a siren leading me to my death—and type out what could be the most dangerous message I've ever sent.

> **Me:** I'll be there at eight to check out the fireplace.

· · · ● · ● ● · ●

Lennon's gravel driveway stretches for what feels like a mile, something I'm sure will be a fantastic selling point when she finally gets the business off the ground.

The white house stretches toward a gray autumn sky. The last time I'd been here, Lennon had a small child running around, baking cookies, and completing puzzles on the living room floor. I'd thought Lennon to be somewhat harsh–certainly not the type to enjoy children. But the woman can make an old, run-down house a home.

I like that about her, I guess.

Possibly too much if last night indicated anything.

I tap the steering wheel aimlessly, trying to diffuse some of the buzzing energy I can't seem to get away from. Everything I did last night did nothing to alleviate whatever feelings have awoken.

I can chalk it up to lust–an annoying desire that needs to get out of my system. Despite confessing the history of my love life to Lennon and seeing her in a new light, we hardly know each other. The details she has of my past are vague–just a loose outline of what happened with Alexis and how it related to the art show last spring.

There've been no heart-to-hearts, no dates–nothing. This is all just a hopeless attraction that I can't seem to squash–a desperate need to get closer to her. Playing with fire, I suppose.

When I put the car in park, I notice the quick closing of the living room curtain and chuckle.

She was waiting for me.

The door opens.

"About time. You're five minutes late."

Lennon stands leaning in the doorway, hair loose and wild, a cup of coffee in her hand. I can't help but remember the images I conjured last night.

Fuck.

"Sorry," I say, stepping up onto the porch. "I had to become a chimney expert overnight."

One eyebrow quirks up as she pins me with those green eyes, her coffee cup hovering close to her lips. "Think you got it figured out?"

I offer her a cocky grin. "Most definitely." I look around, noting the puzzle tucked neatly beneath the coffee table. "No special guests this time?" I ask.

Lennon rolls her eyes as she turns away, striding toward the fireplace. "I was just helping Ellis and her aunt out since I have time off to deal with all this." She waves a hand when she says it before taking another sip of coffee.

"You seemed to enjoy it," I comment. "The cookies smelled good."

She chuckles. "They were contaminated. Caught Eloise eating peanut butter right out of the jar. I'm now short the most common of all the nut butters."

I cough, turning away to hide whatever may be written across my face. Walking to the fireplace, I stare at it. I have the vaguest idea of a plan. "I heard your story about the fairies under the stairs." I kneel, noting the black soot caked on the inside of the brick.

"I like stories," she admits. "I've been trying to figure out what stories this house holds. It's older, and I'm certain there's *something*. However, nobody documents the everyday lives of everyday people. So, I figured I'd make something up."

I turn back to look at her, still standing with her eyes narrowed as if she's assessing my skill level for this particular job. "You added fairies," I point out. "That's not exactly everyday lore."

Lennon raises a shoulder. "It is for a five-year-old."

I smile, turning back to the old brick. "Yeah," I say. "I suppose you're right."

Seven

Lennon

"Any updates?"

I make my way to the rug sprawled over the wooden floors of my living room, sitting down with my almost empty second cup of coffee.

There was no way I could sit in here and watch Noah work, talking about fairies and cookies. He showed up wearing another one of his stupid knit sweaters, his glasses, and an expensive-looking watch. I damn near buckled at the knees.

"Well, you're missing the part that keeps animals out," he answers. "So, that would explain the noises you said you were hearing."

"I'm pretty sure they're bats. I've googled everything there is to know, but I've been too afraid to look."

He turns around, an irritating smirk pulling at the corner of his mouth. "And that's why you're making me do this?"

"First of all," I start, "I'm not making you do anything. And second of all, yes."

He huffs a laugh, bending down to grab the flashlight on the edge of the fireplace. I want to question his aversion to denim, and then I think better of it. Whatever he's doing–it's working. His ass looks great, and I begin to question why I believed it made him look too polished–too perfect–to begin with.

Noah flicks on the flashlight and crawls into the fireplace, pointing the light upward.

I set my mug on the rustic coffee table and lean forward to get a better look. "See anything?"

"No, I just–" There's a pause. "Oh, shit." He's out of the fireplace in an instant.

"Oh, shit?" I ask just before hearing something flutter somewhere in the brick chimney.

Noah backs up, nearly tripping over me when I see it–the black *thing* flying out of my fireplace. "Oh, shit!" I yell as my stomach bottoms out. I'm running to the other room, vaguely aware of Noah swatting at the thing as it circles my living room.

I need to think–I need to do anything other than flee the premises and prove that I'm not cut out for the task I've taken on.

A cast-iron skillet sits on my stove, clean and at an adequate temperature for me to pick it up.

Frantically, I carry it into the living room and hand it to Noah, who is understandably yelling as he tries to do something with the creature now loose in my new home.

"Take this!" I yell, handing him the skillet.

"Goddamn it. Could you have picked a heavier piece of cookware?"

The room has descended into chaos, and my heart is pounding faster than the hooves of a horse at the Kentucky Derby.

"Want me to go back in the kitchen and find one?"

Noah grips the handle, keeping his eyes on the bat that's now screeching. "Never mind," he says. "Can you open a door? I'll try to herd him out."

I duck, trying to dodge the flutter of wings. "He's not a cow!"

"Lennon!"

The assertiveness in his voice pushes me to action as I run to the mudroom, quickly opening the door while Noah swats at the thing–something the bat does not enjoy.

It flies down the hallway to the kitchen, both of us on its tail.

"The sliding door!" I yell, hoping he can *herd* the thing there.

Noah grunts, ducking behind the counter when the creature swoops lower. "A little busy," he says before bouncing back up.

I race to the door, bumping my hip into the small breakfast table and knocking over a vase of flowers before grabbing the handle.

The slide of the door feels like hope just as Noah sprints in my direction, frying pan held high and brow furrowed.

He dodges the shards as the bat flies out, and I slam the sliding door, rattling the entire house before the dust finally settles.

Or glass, I should say, because the broken vase fragments litter the floor. The kitchen is a minefield, but at least there are no more bats flying around.

I look up, panting. "Was that the only one you saw in there?"

Noah places the pan on the floor, his hands on his knees, as he tries to catch his breath. "How am I supposed to know?" He looks up at the ceiling as if he's praying to whatever god will listen. "Holy shit."

My eyes flick to the blooming spot on his sweater, the darkened hue near his wrist.

"Are you–" I squint, making sure my vision isn't failing me. "Noah, are you bleeding?"

He looks down. "What?"

Careful of the glass, I pad in my socks over to him, ripping the arm of his sweater higher until it's pushed above his elbow. There, on his forearm, is a long scratch and two small dots.

"Oh my God, do you even feel that?" I'm careful not to press on it, wondering how he didn't notice that the damn thing bit and scratched him.

"You know," he says, his nose wrinkling. "Now that you mention it, that kind of stings."

"We need to clean it. You probably have rabies or something." I wince. "You probably need to be seen by a doctor."

"First of all, I don't have rabies."

"That we know of," I interrupt, one corner of my mouth lifting. My fingers are still on his arm, the heat settling into my bones.

"That we know of," he says, matching my smile with one of his own. "Second of all, you're probably right." His smile falls, and there's a brief pause. "And I feel sick."

He sways a little, his face pale as I move to catch him, certain that if he goes down, I'll be unsuccessful. "Yeah, okay," I say in a rush. "Come on, Batman. Let's go."

· · · ● · ● · ● · · ·

"Why don't I just drop you off at the front, and I'll go park."

I circle the parking lot again, desperate to find a spot. I don't know if the lot is just small, or if mercury is in retrograde and that's why everyone seems to be injured.

Either way, there are no spots save for the ones miles away from the door.

"Sure," Noah says.

Save for Noah's subtle pallor, nobody would suspect a bat had just flown from a chimney to bite his arm. He looks as if he might throw up.

I glance sidelong at him again, hoping that vomiting isn't in his future. I don't feel like cleaning out my car so soon. "You doing okay?" I ask, tone gentle.

"Yeah, I'm fine. It's fine." He clears his throat, resting his head on the back of the seat as I throw the car into park by the doors.

"Listen," I start, turning to face him. The guilt is there–slowly simmering and reminding me I'm the one who asked him to help. "You don't have to clean out the fireplace for me. I can hire someone."

The small smile he cracks settles something in me. "You would hire someone besides me? I'm clearly the most qualified for the job. Great with chimneys, in fact."

I laugh, realizing that despite the circumstances, I'm quite enjoying myself. Seeing him less polished–more relaxed–only serves to increase my interest. I might actually enjoy getting to know him–spending time with him.

"Bats probably complicate the situation. I'm sure you're fantastic with chimneys, but I think it may be better if you stick to toilets from now on."

Noah chuckles and gets out of the car, leaving me to navigate the parking lot of doom for another ten minutes before I settle on a very long walk to the front door as opposed to waiting for a spot to open up.

When I get into the ER, Noah is nowhere to be found.

I walk up to the desk. "Did Noah Ashwood already go back?"

"Excuse me?" The brunette looks up at me over a pair of quirky glasses–red and green–like a watermelon. "Can I ask your relation?"

Fuck.

They won't let me in if I'm just a–

What am I even?

"His wife," I answer as she runs a pale hand across her keyboard.

Oh God. I could have settled for cousin. What the *fuck* am I doing calling myself his wife in order to get into an Emergency Room with him?

His ride would have been a better description.

I swallow, my cheeks burning hot. *No. Not his ride.*

Without looking at me, she types something into the computer. "He just went back. I can have someone walk you, if you'd like."

My foot taps nervously on the floor–keeping time with the rapid pace of my heart. I hate lying, but I'm in deep, so I might as well own it. "That would be great." I glance around the waiting area. "The parking lot was really full for it to be so empty here."

There's one woman sitting in a chair across the room with her legs crossed and reading glasses perched on the edge of her nose. I strain my neck, trying to catch a glimpse of what she's reading before I'm interrupted by the receptionist again.

"It's been pretty dead today." She offers me her first smile, and it stretches across her face as if she's trying it on for the first time. "Our parking garage is under construction. It moved everyone to this lot. I find it keeps some of the more–" She pauses, trying to find the right word. "Ridiculous cases away."

The doors open, and she gestures toward the nurse waiting–a petite woman who looks much friendlier than the receptionist. "She can take you on back."

When the receptionist explains who I am, calling me the wife of room 156, the nurse's face falls for a moment. Her dark eyes drag to me as a friendly smile returns to her face. "Right this way," she says.

I walk just behind her–too nervous to make small talk for fear I'll ruin my cover.

She gestures to the door, her warm brown skin glowing like the smile she wears. "You're husband's in here. Should be quick, considering what happened. We're just waiting on the doctor."

"Thanks," I say, trying to match her tone and failing miserably. I crack the door open and poke my head in. "Hi," I say, before glancing at the nurse behind me. "Honey," I add–just for good measure.

Noah's face twists into confusion.

The nurse clears her throat–her friendly demeanor turning uncomfortable. "I'll leave you and your wife for a moment. The doctor should be in soon."

"Yes, thank you!" The words come out in a rush–a desperate attempt to keep Noah from contradicting my lie.

I move to the chair next to the bed and chuckle. "Nice gown," I say.

Sterile equipment and an overwhelming amount of white decorate the small room in the ER. The receptionist had been right, everything seems relatively quiet today. I tap a finger on the metal arm of the uncomfortable chair to burn off some energy.

He doesn't smile. His brows furrow, and he leans in–lowering his voice. "Wife?" he questions.

"Shut up," I respond. "They're going to suspect something, and the receptionist asked my relation." I wave a hand. "I had to think of something quickly."

"Lennon–"

"I didn't think they'd let me in!" My voice comes out defensive-loud-squeaky.

Noah laughs-the sound burrowing beneath my skin and soothing like a balm. I don't normally question my actions this much, but something about how relaxed he'd been at my house-his proximity-it's all working together to mess with my mind. "Of course they'd let you in," he says, shaking his head.

I wince, glancing at the door before back at him. "I wasn't taking any chances." The fear of the doctor coming in grips me, and I scramble-convinced we need to be putting on a convincing show. The best way for me to get over any weirdness is to really lean into my decisions. "Act loving," I demand.

Noah deadpans. "No."

"Oh, come on." I push back in the chair casually as a memory flashes, unbidden, in my mind. "It's not like I'm asking you to casually make out with me." I roll my eyes for emphasis, and there it is. The sting that returns. The reason, presumably, that I've become more nervous in his presence-less sure of myself.

Noah runs his tongue along his teeth before responding, and I can't help but think about what it would be like-to kiss him. I bet he'd be good at it-an expert, really.

"I was flirting with the nurse," he admits, and I laugh, tipping my head back.

"No, you were not!"

"It's not funny."

I smile then. "Yes, it is. That poor girl." I can't help the small thread of discomfort that rests heavily in the pit of my stomach. I'm just reminded of the rejection.

Noah will flirt with the nurse he just met while sitting in a hospital gown, looking equal parts hot and ridiculous. He throws himself at women—tons of them.

Not me.

I fight the urge to grimace. I've never been known as someone who cares—never let it show, at least, and I'm not about to start now.

"Well, you've ruined my chances," he says, shifting uncomfortably on the bed.

"Oh, please." I tap the arm of the chair, keeping a grin on my face. The sterile scent of the hospital doesn't exactly say *romance*. It seems like the worst place to pick up a woman. "Your chances were already ruined."

<h1 style="text-align:center">Eight</h1>

Noah

My grip tightens on the sweater in my hand as we trek across the parking lot to wherever Lennon parked, and I can't help but be embarrassed about the entire situation.

There's a small patch of dried blood painted on the sleeve of my sweater, making me grateful for the black t-shirt I had been wearing beneath it. My fingers trace over the bandage on my arm–the bite now stinging as the cool air pebbles my skin.

I can't believe a bat fucking bit me.

I had to get a rabies shot at the ER.

And I'll have to go in for more than just one shot in the coming days.

Lennon folds her arms across her chest to fight off the cold, keeping her eyes firmly fixed on the horizon. For what it's worth, after she animatedly rehashed the entire story to the doctor, Lennon was also required to get a rabies shot–just in case.

She didn't seem upset about my admission to flirting with the nurse, either. I'll confess I feel bad for the woman. I'd laid the charm on pretty thick prior to Lennon's arrival, and I was certain the nurse was into it. Unfortunately, our budding romance–or whatever the fuck you'd call it–was thwarted by the arrival of my *wife*.

I've never appeared more sleazy.

Casual hook-ups and blatant unfaithfulness are two very separate things. The former, I've grown quite accustomed to, but the latter makes bile rise in my throat.

I check my watch, noting that my entire morning has slipped by, and we are now firmly sitting in the late afternoon. I've wasted my entire day off in her presence, but framing it as a *waste* seems inaccurate.

I'd spent months trying to get close to Lennon to apologize, but now that I'm here, I've realized she's not so difficult to understand. Lennon's not some pompous classic novel riddled with complex figurative language–meanings so convoluted any literary scholar who claims to understand the author's intent is just inventing shit. She resembles reading for pleasure–getting lost in a story so thoroughly you forget how much time has gone by. Still complex but far more enjoyable.

She reminds me of all the reasons I chose my profession to begin with—the fun parts.

"Your chimney's still not fixed," I say to break the silence.

When I glance sidelong at her, I notice the way she pulls part of her lip in her mouth—biting gently. Her brows lowered in contemplation as Lennon refuses to look at me.

Fuck, I wish she'd look at me the way she had earlier when we were laughing in the ER about her grotesque reenactment of what might have been the closest I've ever come to becoming a superhero.

I'd always preferred Spiderman, but Batman happens to be a close second.

"I'm not worried," she says, wrapping her arms tighter around herself.

I glance at my sweater and wince, holding it up to make my point. "I'd give you this, but I'm afraid there's still some dried blood on the sleeve."

Lennon laughs as if I've said something ridiculous. "I don't need your damn sweater, Noah."

She unfolds her arms, still focused on her steps and whatever's ahead. "I'll hire a professional for the chimney," she says. "I'm not worried about *that*. However, I hate shots, and I will be sleeping in a house with bats until it's fixed."

One corner of my mouth turns up. "Suits your personality."

"Shut up," she says, but there's no malice in her tone. She looks at me, a smile cracking across her face, and I'm thankful we've returned to the casual banter. *God,* she looks good like this.

"You could–" I pause. It's a fruitless attempt to stop myself from saying the rest of what I'm inevitably about to say. I know I'm going to regret this later. "I have a couch."

It's barely an offer.

Lennon cocks an eyebrow in my direction. "No guest room?"

I shrug, fighting the embarrassment that threatens to call me out. After Alexis, I didn't see a need for more space–another bedroom. Somehow, Lennon's question feels deeper–like she could discern too much from my answer.

"Cheaper to buy a one-bedroom house." I offer. It's a half-truth.

A smirk dances on her lips as we stand next to her car. "And you'd let me stay over?" she asks.

I turn toward her, raising a brow in challenge. "I don't see why not."

That smile still rests on her face. "I can think of plenty of reasons why not."

I gape at Lennon as she reaches in her back pocket for her buzzing phone. When she glances at the screen, she grimaces. I briefly catch the *Dad* caller ID before she's glancing up at me. "I am going to take this," she states before sliding her finger across the screen and stepping away.

I hear the car door unlock as Lennon places herself on the other side of the SUV parked next to us, but I don't move to get inside.

"It's going well." I hear her say before she chuckles–her tone tight. I lean against the back of the car, pulling my phone out and scrolling through my emails. I might as well use my time wisely–answering students while I wait.

After a moment, Lennon returns, her phone still held to her ear as she nods toward the car and starts climbing inside.

"Yeah," she says as I open the door to the passenger seat and get in. "There was a bat issue, but it's being resolved."

When both doors are closed, Lennon starts the engine, and I can hear what's being said on the other line. I'm not sure I'm supposed to. "I still think you should give this up, Lennon." The man's tone sounds scolding. "You're being foolish. It's time to stop chasing the fanciful. Your sister is in a stable relationship with a stable profession—one that speaks of her intelligence. I want the same for you."

Lennon glances warily in my direction before her grip tightens on her phone as she backs out of the parking spot. Clearing her throat, she appears visibly uncomfortable. "I don't want to be a doctor, Dad."

My brow furrows at the shift in her tone. She sounds weak, and if I know anything about Lennon, it's that she is nothing of the sort. The woman on the phone is not the same woman who demanded I make out with her. It's not the same woman who called herself my wife just to get into the ER. Everything about her has shifted with one phone call. When I look up from my email inbox, I can see it, too. She's gone cold—her spark dying like whatever he's said has completely snuffed out her flame.

I shift uncomfortably in my seat.

"I have to go," she says.

When she finally hangs up, I don't say a word. I'm not sure what I *should* say. I feel as if I've intruded on a conversation I wasn't meant to hear—seen something I wasn't meant to see.

"Sorry." Lennon leans forward, turning her blinker on as she changes lanes.

I can't keep my eyes off her. It's like I need to take in every subtle shift in her demeanor and take notes on how to fix it. There's so much I've yet to uncover about this woman, but I know for damn sure that whatever is sitting next to me–it isn't *her*. I'm used to brash insults, not apologies. "What are you saying sorry for?" I ask.

Lennon keeps her hands fixed to the wheel. "You overheard that. Weird vibes. I was saying sorry."

"Don't apologize."

When she glances my direction, those green eyes hold my stare for a moment, widening before she looks away. "Okay," she whispers.

I've spent a lot of time with women since Alexis, and not once have I felt this ache in my chest or this pit in my stomach. It's like I need to do something about whatever the fuck is wrong with her, but unfortunately for me–Lennon only shares what she wants. While she's forthright with quite a lot, there are layers of vulnerability beneath the surface, and I don't think asking will get me answers. She has to tell me on her own.

I settle for a change in topic. "Do we need to pick things up from the Inn?"

"What?" she questions.

I adjust my glasses, keeping my tone casual. "You're staying on my couch, correct?"

Lennon flushes, the subtle shade of pink sending a thrill through my blood.

"I mean," I continue, cracking a smile. "Unless the bats are your thing–"

"We can pick up a few things."

The corner of her mouth quirks up, and the banter settles some of that aching feeling. I still want to know why she shut down. What the fuck is wrong with the career she's chosen to pursue?

Lennon is far from unsuccessful. She's the same age as Griffin's girl–meaning she's still in her twenties. The fact that she's done as much as she has screams success and determination.

The girl bought a fucking bed-and-breakfast.

It's far beyond what I've been able to accomplish in my early thirties. Sure, I bought a house, but it's about twelve square feet away from qualifying as a tiny home, something my mother hates. She believes I was shortsighted–that I needed space to start a family.

I didn't have the heart to tell her that dream was dead.

I barely have the space to host a girl who is trying to escape the bats in her chimney.

"I'll have you know," I start. "There are no strange animals living in my house."

Lennon laughs, resting her head on the back of the seat. "Odd, considering *you* live there."

• • ● ● • ● ● • •

We stopped at the Inn to grab a few things before I gave Lennon directions to my house.

I usually avoid giving women my address, let alone inviting them to sleep on my couch. If I were going to invite a woman over, I'd probably recommend sleeping in the bed–with me. But even then, it's rare that I open my space to someone else. I find it blurs the line of what I establish very clearly in my relationships.

Sex. Nothing else.

Lennon could never be *that*, though. With our ties to Griffin and Ellis, maintaining the appropriate boundaries for a purely physical relationship would be nearly impossible.

Especially when it feels like she's finally letting me see more of her. I *want* her in my space, but as I unlock the deadbolt and open the door, my stomach twists.

Lennon walks in before me, looking around as if she's searching for a flaw. I'm hyper-aware as I realize how impersonal my home is. The bed-and-breakfast may be falling apart, but at least the house has character. My house feels stiff–cold.

I've worked hard to create a *nice* space, but it's hardly a home, and something about that makes me feel self-conscious.

I close the door behind us with a soft *snick*.

"Well," she starts, scanning the warm beige and cream hues found on the walls and the accent pillows.

Well?"

When Lennon turns, the light has returned to her eyes, and I'm thankful. Whatever weird cloud made its home over her head after she spoke with her father freaked me out.

"It's clean," she observes.

I raise a brow. "What did you expect?"

She smiles, sharp like a knife, and damn if it doesn't do something to me. "Well, I wasn't expecting curtains and accent pillows. A bachelor pad should scream *man*. I'm guessing you don't have a headboard."

"What does that have to do with–"

She's gone, stomping down the hallway on a mission to find I don't know what. My secrets? The aforementioned headboard, perhaps?

"Where are you going?" I trail behind her until she practically kicks down the door to my bedroom and lets herself in.

Her head tilts to the side as she takes in the queen-sized bed with my comforter neatly sprawled across the mattress. There's a second disorganized bookshelf in the corner, the only thing I fail to keep neat and organized.

When she turns around, her body framed by the background of my bed, I can't help but let my mind wander. I've conjured up enough images of Lennon sprawled out on my mattress that it's difficult to keep them from flashing in my mind with her standing so close.

"You *do* have a headboard. A bedframe, too. I'm impressed, Mr. English Professor." She smirks before chewing on her lip, as if she longs to keep the smile from growing too wide.

"She's impressed." I lean in, just slightly. "Though I'm afraid your expectations were far too low. You seem surprised I own a bed at all. Where did you think I slept?" I ask. "In a coffin next to my bats, like you?"

Her smile breaks free. "Ha, ha. Very funny."

"Why are we standing in my bedroom, Lennon?" I shove my hands in my pockets, leaning back on my heels.

Her nose scrunches up, and she glances away. "Right." Her cheeks pink—a soft color I'd love to make deepen. "Your bedroom is open to all but me."

I tilt my head, brows pulling together. "I don't invite many women into my bedroom."

She pins me with her stare, her eyes flaming with challenge. "So, I'm good enough to see your bed, but you're unwilling to kiss me."

I swallow, the silence stretching between us—thick and heavy. When my smile drops from my face, my gaze flicks to her pink lips—full and gently parted.

I step forward, noting the way she sucks in a breath. "I'm surprised," I admit. Her green eyes remain unwavering, and I suddenly want to rise to whatever challenge she's throwing my way. Does she still want me to kiss her?

Would it be so bad if the lines blurred a little?

The faint scent of mint surrounds me, her breath hot and close—so close. "I didn't think you'd be one to beg."

Lennon lifts her chin, my eyes dropping to her mouth just briefly. "I would *never* beg," she asserts.

A corner of my mouth turns up, my resolve pleasantly absent. I want her. I want her honesty, her barbs, her laugh.

Fuck.

"So, you're not begging?" I question, my fingers finding the smooth skin of her wrist, gently encircling it on instinct. The desire to pull her closer consumes me. "What would you call this, then?"

Finally, her eyes drop for a moment, the longing driving me to the brink of insanity. "Kiss me," she says.

All the blood rushes to my cock at her words.

She still wants this, and I'm too far gone to consider the consequences.

"Not begging?" I question, my voice low.

Her lips brush mine—just briefly. "I'm not," she whispers. "I'm demanding."

I make a decision—a fucking stupid one, but I'll worry about that part later.

I kiss her. She stiffens at first, giving me a moment to second-guess everything before she finally melts into me, soft lips pressing to mine as she fists her hands in my shirt and tugs me forward. I tangle my hands in her hair in response, desperate to pull her closer.

Drunk on her sharp inhale and the way she presses into me, I trace her bottom lip with my tongue. She tastes like cinnamon and apples—like the autumn outside. I'm not sure I know what I'm doing at this point. Making out with Lennon shouldn't be complicated—it's not as if she were offering me a relationship, and she knows my history better than most women I've hooked up with. So why, oh why, does it feel so fucking different when her lips part and her tongue meets mine?

My hand tightens in her hair, pulling gently before I walk her back until she's against the wall. The grind of her hips, the contact. It pulls a groan from deep in my chest.

I'm all too aware of how fucking hard I am, and suddenly aware of how reckless this is.

Our lives are too entangled. There's no getting *out* with Lennon. No way to escape her if things become too much–if someone starts feeling something.

I move my hand, slowly gliding it until it rests gently around her throat. I run my thumb over her soft skin there and note the rapid pulse beneath my fingers before grinding myself against her, chasing friction as she groans into my mouth.

Swallowing the sound, I do it again–getting the same result, and suddenly, I'm high on it.

It's not enough. Kissing her isn't enough.

I'm greedy for her. I want her soft panting in my ear. I want Lennon to chant my name. There's so much about her I want–too much. The way she unabashedly says what's on her mind, her sense of humor, the banter–all of it. I could drown in this woman.

Fuck.

What am I doing?

I break the kiss, pulling back and noting the heat in her gaze. It's enough to make my knees weak and solidify the fact that this was a terrible fucking idea.

Lennon isn't Charlie, or Julia. She's not like any of the women I've slept with, and that makes this far too dangerous.

I've bent so many rules with her already. Mutual friends, fixing her house, inviting her to *mine.*

This can't happen again–it won't.

One corner of my mouth turns up in an expression so opposite of everything I'm feeling, it seems like I'm lying to her face.

"There," I say. "You wanted to make out. You got what you asked for." I step back, trying to fight off the bile rising in my throat—the uncomfortable feelings raging in my gut. "That was that. We won't be doing it again."

I step back, hoping like hell she doesn't look down to where my cock strains in my pants. I roll my tongue along my teeth before clearing my throat. "Make yourself at home."

And then I leave her there.

Nine

Lennon

"How do you continue a casual conversation with some-one while staying at their house after making out with them?"

"Oh, hello, Lennon." Ellis has the wherewithal to seem unfazed by the unannounced video call and unhinged question, but Cass's jaw is on the floor. Actually, it might be in hell.

Cass pauses her walk down the busy street, the city lights illuminating her blonde hair as it whips around. "I beg your pardon," she says. "What did you just ask?"

I look up, noting the fan in Noah's bathroom is loud, but it doesn't seem loud enough for this conversation. Standing from where I placed myself on the floor, I turn the sink on, hoping the water will drown out my conversation.

This probably should have waited.

After Noah left me standing in his bedroom, I didn't really know what to do. I've never been stunned silent before, except maybe when my father is talking to me about passions and career trajectories. That will shut me up pretty quickly.

Aside from that, I always have something to say–always.

Not this time.

When Noah disappeared down the hall, the fog of whatever his kiss had done to me finally lifted. Reality crashed into me, realizing how forward I'd been–desperate. Embarrassment burned hot in my blood as I analyzed everything that followed that kiss.

He'd vowed kissing wouldn't happen again and had no qualms when it came to leaving me alone in his bedroom. The entire interaction reminded me of everything I've heard about him.

If casual is a requirement, I'll slap that shit on my resume and apply because the man can *kiss*.

I didn't know where to go from his bedroom, and since his house is nowhere near the size of the bed-and-breakfast, I scurried to the bathroom, locked the door, and sent out an SOS via Facetime.

If Noah could be cool and unrattled after a kiss like that, so could I.

I return to my spot on the bathroom floor. "I'm just wondering," I start. "If you were to make out with someone–"

Ellis settles on the couch, popping a chip in her mouth and asking her question around it. "Did you go on a date with this person?" she asks.

"No, it's casual."

Cass chuckles as she keeps walking. "Everything seems very casual. Casual conversation, casual making out. Who is this theoretical guy?"

No sense in hiding it. "It's Noah, but that's beside the point."

Ellis chokes on a chip, and her eyes flick away from the screen to catch on someone who is with her. My eyes narrow, knowing exactly who she is with.

"Wait, did she say Noah?" Griffin's deep voice comes out of my phone speaker, and I realize I've fucked up. He's best friends with Noah. This is already a mess.

I roll my eyes. "Your relationship is ruining my life, Ellis. Hi, Griffin."

His face pops up on the screen as he sits next to her, wrapping an arm around her shoulders and pulling her closer. "Lennon," he says, inviting himself to this panicked group Facetime call from the inside of the bathroom.

Lovely.

"If I made out with Noah for some weird fucking reason, how should I go about acting normal after the fact."

"Acting normal?" Ellis questions. "How did this even happen, for starters? Why are you at his house? Was this premeditated? What is going on?"

I lean back against the sink cabinets, holding my phone aloft. "None of that is relevant. It was an accident–I think. He started it." I chew on my thumbnail as the water continues to run behind me. He's probably going to murder me for this month's water bill. "Well, technically, I asked for it."

Griffin shifts to pull his phone from his back pocket, and for the first time in my life, I think I have a mini panic attack.

"Don't text him!" I screech.

He looks up, brows furrowing before he sets his phone aside. "Sorry, I was just trying to get the full story here," Griffin chimes in. "Don't you hate him?"

"Yes." No? "I shouldn't have gotten everyone involved."

Cass walks off the street, her microphone clearly muted as she enters what appears to be a bar. When she unmutes it, country music blasts through the speakers. "You summoned a whole committee for this, Lennon." She presses a button, and her line goes silent.

"So, I did."

"And you're still at his house?" Ellis asks.

It's official. I'm being crazy.

I've never had a one-night stand before. I've had a handful of relationships at varying levels of seriousness, but I'm not under the impression Noah does anything serious–except maybe sticking his tongue down throats. He seemed incredibly serious when he shoved it down my throat. He was very skilled.

I'm not even sure what I *want* from all of this. There's no future, but I can admit that I like Noah–as a person. He's funny, intelligent, fucking hot.

It would have been the right move to think everything through before I asked him to kiss me... again.

I can feel my cheeks flush, probably obvious to the committee I've summoned. "Yes," I say. "I am. I should probably go. There were bats in my chimney, and he was helping out. It's very complicated, and I'll have to explain later."

Cass unmutes her microphone again. "We can all get coffee or something later. Maybe we can come by the bed-and-breakfast to discuss next weekend."

"I've been wanting to do a bonfire thing," I say. "You're right. We will discuss later. Don't fucking text him, Griffin. You're on my side."

His brow furrows. "There are sides?"

"Yes." I hear a sound on the other side of the door and stand up. "Okay, everyone, meeting over."

Hanging up my phone, I quickly shut off the water, turn the fan off, and open the door. Noah stands there with one brow cocked and his fist raised as if he were about to knock.

"Everything alright?" he asks.

"Yeah." I wipe my hands on my pants. "I actually forgot my bag. I'm going to change."

"About earlier–"

Oh god. Kissing him back was a terrible idea. The worst idea I've had to date. Worse than staying in Ohio after college to get away from my family's judgment–something that hadn't worked at all. My father and sister are fully capable of judging my life choices from states away.

And when it comes to Noah Ashwood, I'm fully capable of wanting more.

The man chased a bat out of my house, ended up receiving one of multiple rabies shots, and not once was he upset with me. He didn't judge the bed-and-breakfast idea. He's shown nothing but kindness, and something about that is messing with my head.

"It didn't mean anything," I say, my tone coming out bored. If I'm good at anything, it is not showing my true emotions. Shrugging, I skirt around him, finding my backpack left by the front door and slinging it over my shoulder. I packed some leggings and a sweatshirt to sleep in.

Noah blocks my return to his restroom, towering over me as his dark eyes bore into mine. "Right. I don't do relationships."

I can feel my face scrunch up. What does he think? I'm in love with him or something?

I laugh it off. "I know that, Noah. I'm not an idiot. It was just a kiss." A good fucking kiss, and he knows it too, or he wouldn't be clarifying right now.

He rubs the back of his neck nervously. "Good, I'm glad we're on the same page. I meant what I said, though." He's not wearing his glasses but still has the same outfit on from earlier–minus the sweater. "We can't do it again. There are too many complications–our lives are too entwined. But I'd like to be friends."

I blink.

This is an odd speech.

I was under no false impressions that Noah was doing anything more than kissing me. I've liked having him around–arguing with him. That doesn't mean that I'm expecting anything from him. Maybe I'm just a little hurt over the art show last spring and needing an outlet. I've been on a few dates over the summer, but nothing memorable. Then Noah came in, asking to fix my toilet. He took everything I threw at him and didn't balk. Instead of deeming me a failure for doing this *thing* and buying the house, he came in and offered to help with things he knew nothing about.

He was trying to help last spring when he chased off my date.

Deep down, Noah is a lot more than his fear of relationships or whatever this is, but I know better than to hope that he'd see me as special or different. I'm not the one that will change his mind.

I realize I haven't answered. "Sure. You can come to the bonfire at the house next weekend, Friend." My grip tightens on my backpack. "I just started planning it, and I'm inviting Ellis, Cass, and maybe some others. Griffin will be invited. It'll be a party, I suppose."

"Great." He smiles.

"Great."

The silence that follows is deafening and uncomfortable. I can't help but fill it.

"Do you want to watch a movie?" I ask, and Noah raises his brows. "As friends."

Clearing his throat, Noah shifts where he stands. His eyes flick toward the living room before one corner of his mouth turns up. "What do you want to watch?"

I shrug, pushing past him to change into my more comfortable clothes. "Something nobody has heard of," I toss over my shoulder. "We can surf whatever streaming service you have when I'm done."

· · · ● ● · ● ● · · ·

Noah had gotten a plate together of fancy cheeses, crackers, fruit, and meat while I was changing and had it ready and waiting when I returned. We settled on a mystery thriller about a detective getting involved with a former cold case and uncovering dark secrets, and so far, the film is exactly something I'd be interested in.

Minus the jump scares.

"I didn't think you'd be the type to freak out every time something jumps out." Noah's voice trails over my skin, making goosebumps rise.

"I'm not freaked out," I say, wrapping my arms around my torso and fixing my eyes to the screen. When I bring my legs up onto the couch, knees as close to my chest as I can get them, I'm not sure I'm convincing Noah of anything.

"Sure," he says, and I risk glancing in his direction. He's still wearing the same outfit from earlier, and I can't help but wonder what he sleeps in. Slacks? It's hard to picture him in anything else. "You only leap five feet off the couch every time a very predictable jump scare occurs."

I stretch my leg across the small sectional and push against his leg, feeling nothing but firm muscle beneath. "I am *not* jumping five feet off the couch." The phantom of his kiss passes over my mouth, my lips tingling with the memory. My cheeks heat, and I run my finger over the edge of one of Noah's fancy pillows. The embroidery decorating the fabric scratches against my skin.

"Are you embarrassed?" he asks.

"No."

He's shifting closer as I draw my legs back. The only thing I'm scared of is the warmth of his nearness as he places himself right next to me, miles of couch sprawling behind him. *God*, it's like the kiss did nothing to settle my attraction to the man. If anything, it only awakened a beast inside of me. A beast that absolutely *must* be ovulating.

Noah brings his face closer to mine, a smile forming on his lips. "Your cheeks are turning red. You're definitely embarrassed." He leans back but keeps himself close enough to touch, turning to face the television again. "The jump scares are predictable, Lennon. I'm surprised someone like you would fall for it."

"Someone like me?" I ask, unsure of his meaning. "And what am I, Noah?"

Those dark eyes flick in my direction, one brow cocked as he lifts his arm to rest on the back of the couch. Luckily, I'm still pressed against the corner of the sectional facing him, or his arm would be around me.

"Intelligent," he finally responds. The smile falls from his face, his brows lowering in the dim lights of his living room. "Stalwart and passionate." He looks away, focusing on the movie once more, but I'm no longer watching.

Something warms in my chest at the words he chose to describe me. Of course they mean nothing–Noah hardly knows me, but still, the contrast between what he's said and what my father has told me is obvious. I've been called foolish, fanciful, difficult, selfish. None of those words are positive—nothing like *stalwart* or *intelligent*.

Despite my best efforts to keep my vulnerability hidden, I test the waters, scoffing. "Selfish, maybe. Impulsive."

Noah looks at me again, and it feels like he is looking right through me, concern etched into every wrinkle as he tries to discern my meaning. "You bought the bed-and-breakfast." he says. "Planned what you'd do. Budgeted. Went after exactly what you wanted."

I don't understand where he's going with this. "Yeah," I say.

"Someone hand you that money overnight?"

Rude. I'm sure he sees the look of disgust on my face, but he doesn't pull back. "No. I made sacrifices. I saved."

Noah leans closer, his eyes running from my gaze to the tips of my toes and back up. It's almost painful to be seen like this. I don't like my insecurities laid out so plainly. "That's hardly impulsive." He leans away again, and I'm not sure if I'm enjoying the odd push and pull or if it is driving me mad.

Probably both.

Noah continues, "and entering hospitality as a career path is hardly *selfish*. You'll be serving other people."

He leaves it at that, lost in the movie again and not acknowledging me at all.

The man *just* gave me a speech about how he doesn't do relationships. I assured him it was just a kiss, but I now see the danger of Noah Ashwood. It's not just that he's attractive. It's that he's perceptive, funny, and kind. It'd be easy to lose myself in him.

"Is this about what my dad said on the phone?" I ask, and by his short *humph* and the way he won't look at me, I know it has to be true.

I let myself relax more into the cushions, spreading out until my foot is just touching him as I turn to watch the TV.

"Thanks," I almost whisper.

Noah taps the top of the couch where his hand is still resting. "Just telling the truth."

A small smile plays on my lips, and when a little girl jumps out in front of the protagonist, combined with the creepiest music I've ever heard. I don't even jump.

Ten

Noah

"Another one?"

Lennon sprawls across my couch as the credits run across the screen, casting my living room in dim light and nothing more. The sun descended on the horizon a while ago, and in the darkness, I migrated closer to her, her socked feet propped on my lap.

While I've uncovered certain layers of Lennon's life–pieces I'm not entirely sure she wanted me to see–there's still something so open about her. Without hesitation, she relaxed into my space. The blush on her cheeks, her expressiveness, the way she asks for what she wants? It all feels so refreshing.

With Alexis, I spent plenty of time guessing, but with Lennon, I don't feel the need to guess. Even the layers I haven't uncovered don't feel secretive, just private—sacred. It leaves me longing to remain in her orbit—if only for the small chance she'll offer me a small piece of herself.

"Another movie?" I clarify, nodding once in agreement. "Sure, what are you feeling?"

Sitting up, she withdraws every part of her that made contact, and I hate it. "Another one nobody has heard of before," she says. "It's more fun that way." When she smiles, it's warm—genuine—revealing yet another side to the woman who has been popping in and out of my life for the past nine months. When Griffin and Ellis started dating, we ran in the same circle. Seeing each other in passing—the art show. It's weird to think I've waited this long to have a genuine conversation with her.

I look at the nearly empty plate of food sitting on the ottoman and snag a cracker before speaking. "I need to get you some blankets," I say. "And maybe change, first. Did you want anything else to eat?"

Her smile widens as she leans forward, plucking a cherry from the small bowl sitting on the plate. "This was fine, thanks." When her head tilts to the side, she asks, "Do you cook or just prepare charcuterie boards for every meal?"

I chuckle, relaxing a bit more at the casual conversation. "I cook a bit." I shrug. "My mom loves cooking. She's from Vietnam. Her adoptive parents were white, so she took up cooking as a means to reconnect with her culture." Headlights from a passing car leak in through the curtains, highlighting Lennon's wide green eyes. She leans forward slightly as if she's listening with her entire body. "I like that." I shake my head. "That my mom does that, I mean. At first, she practically forced me to help, claiming it would be important. Now, I actually enjoy it. My dad, on the other hand, can't boil water."

"What are your parents like?" she asks. "Aside from the cooking. Just..." She waves a hand. "In general."

Lennon hugs her knees to her chest, resting her chin there. Her hair falls in a curtain around her shoulders and legs, making her look so at ease. I like her this way, and maybe that's why I don't mind offering up pieces of myself as the night creeps in from outside.

I don't typically sit on my couch with women I've kissed and talk about my family. That's a no-fly zone. I don't invite them to my house, offer my couch, watch movies with them, prepare charcuterie boards, or let them use my lap as their own personal footrest either. But somehow with Lennon, it's all different. It's easy.

"A very standard parent situation," I say. "Or maybe not so much, since my parents are still together and very much in love. I don't think that's the norm." My chest tightens, and I clear my throat.

While working on my doctorate, I'd thought I had what my parents had. It felt like it, anyway. Alexis and I were engaged, en route to a happy marriage complete with kids, a dream home, my career–

When everything crumbled, I'd felt wholly inadequate–as if my incompetence contributed to our demise. I questioned my parent's ability to stay in love–their effortless way of existing with one another. During different periods in my childhood, they'd leaned on one another. When my father lost his job, my mother stepped up. When my mother had been unhappy with hers, my father carried that burden.

It felt... *right*.

Being an only child, there were moments I'd felt alone. The idea of joining my life with another person, supporting one another, enjoying one another–it felt like a good existence. Maybe I romanticized it because that kind of life never found me, and Alexis had made sure to let me know it had been my fault.

But things with Alexis started to feel *hard*. I spent a lot of time guessing what she wanted or how she wanted me to behave.

I'm not thinking about those things with Lennon. If I piss her off, she'll tell me. If I make her feel uncomfortable, I'm certain she'd let me know. She enjoys privacy but not secrecy.

I find myself *wanting* to tell her.

"My parents met in college during one of their freshman classes and have been in love ever since. My dad is a very stereotypical dad all the way down to the bad jokes."

Lennon laughs, and I can feel the sound on my skin like a brand. "And your mom?" she asks.

I smile, my chest warming. "Well, she hated my fiancee, that's for fucking sure." I chuckle softly. "I'm afraid I have a very boring and generally unproblematic family. My impeccable sense of humor comes from other trauma."

Lennon laughs again, softer than before, as she grabs another cherry. "You have a pretty good sense of humor, I suppose. The sheer fact that it goes beyond dick jokes is an accomplishment for the male species."

I grin. "Don't worry. I can also tell a superior dick joke. I'm a *huge* success in that regard."

Lennon raises a brow, the temperature in the room rising slightly. "Are you?" she inquires.

Holding my gaze, her lips wrap around the cherry pinched between her thumb and finger. Now that I'm watching her, I note the way she gently bites the fruit in half. When she brings the fruit back to her mouth and sucks the pit, holding it between her teeth, my heart rate kicks up a notch. It's overtly sexual–or maybe not. Maybe it's all in my head, and the blood pumping faster and rushing to my cock is just my own desire awakening again.

When she discards the center of the cherry on the plate and eats the rest, my brain short circuits.

Holy fuck.

I wince, chastising myself for the way my thoughts shifted. "Um–" I think I was about to explain my parents' college majors, but that seems irrelevant now. All I can think about is kissing her again–tasting the cherry on her lips and running my tongue along hers. The last time we kissed, she tasted like autumn, but I'm wondering if my lips touched hers now, I'd find only summertime. I would love to find out.

Lennon's eyes widen, her pink mouth gently parts as she stares at me, tracking exactly where my gaze fixes.

But I'd like to be friends.

The biggest fucking lie I've ever allowed myself to believe. Apparently, I'd very much like to touch her–something that we've established is not happening.

I stand up abruptly. "Let me get you those blankets and go change. You can pick something out."

"Okay," she whispers.

I turn, quickly retreating to my bedroom and closing the door. I grab a pair of sweatpants and a sweatshirt from the closet, trying to reign my thoughts in before they get out of control. If she were anyone else, I'd do something about the way she was looking at me–but it's *Lennon*. I need to keep reminding myself of that because, for some fucking reason, I forgot earlier.

I should have never put my mouth on hers. She's too addicting.

I pull on my clothes and grab my phone, scrolling to a name–any name. I settle on *Morgan from the Conference* and quickly type out a text.

Me: Hey

God, do I even remember what conference she was from? I know I slept with her. I can picture her face just fine, but how long has it been? Eight months? Nine? I went on a date with her at some point that didn't work out. It was probably around the time Griffin met Ellis.

Why the fuck am I texting her?

When I see the read receipt and no response, I sigh, feeling like the biggest asshole on the planet. I leave the bedroom and grab a flannel blanket from the hall closet.

I'm a mess.

"Here," I say, handing the blanket to Lennon once I'm back in the living room. She has some movie pulled up on the TV. I don't care to look at what it is, but I also can't look at her again.

I check my phone–nothing.

Throwing myself onto the couch, I toss my phone on the ottoman and adjust the hood of my sweatshirt. If Lennon saw this fucking text message, what would she say?

I'm briefly brought back to the moment she thought I was sleeping with someone's *wife*. That kind of judgment from her made my chest feel tight–like I didn't want her to know how royally fucked I am when it comes to relationships, as if she doesn't already know.

When I finally look at her, she wears a questioning look, and my stomach flips. Caught red-handed. Did she see the text?

"What?" I ask.

She shakes her head and chuckles. "Nothing," she says. "I've just never seen you in anything but dress pants." Picking up the remote, Lennon turns on the movie, and I'm thankful for the welcome distraction from the raging hard-on I had ten minutes ago. I need to lose myself in another film full of jump scares and plot twists. I need to stop thinking about the woman in my house–in my head.

"I thought you slept in fancy sweater vests and slacks," she quips while unfolding the flannel blanket I gave her and settling in. "Possibly a full suit."

My mouth quirks up. "Hardly."

Loud panting fills the room as the movie opens with a graphic sex scene that is not the escape I had in mind.

Jesus Christ.

"Shit," I mutter, reaching for the remote and fumbling, frantically trying to make it stop. This is not what we need to be watching.

Lennon laughs when I finally get the movie to pause–a random ass fully displayed on the screen. "What?" she starts. "Are you afraid of a little sex, Noah?"

I grimace, leaning back into the couch.

"No." *Yes.* I'm afraid of what she's doing to me.

"They're just going for shock factor. The movie has a plot. I read the description." She's smiling now, clearly amused at my weird reaction.

I'm an adult and need to act like an adult. I dissociate and let the scene play out, thankful that it ends rather quickly. As the night wears on, we get more comfortable. When Lennon goes to the restroom, I pause the movie, clean up our food, and return to the couch to prop my feet up on the ottoman.

She returns, sitting much closer than I thought she would, and uses the ottoman to sprawl out, too. Grabbing the flannel blanket, she extends it over both of us, slouching down into the cushions like she wouldn't want to be anywhere else.

I'm suddenly aware of what we are doing.

I haven't sat around with a woman in a long time, not since Alexis, and I can't say that I'm upset about it. It's nice having her here, her warmth seeping into me, her thigh resting against mine beneath the flannel blanket. My arm stretches out over the back of the couch, careful not to touch her until her eyes drift closed, and she shifts, leaning her head against my chest. It's only then that I allow my hand to fall to her shoulder, pulling her in closer on instinct.

I tune back into the movie, tracking every place our bodies touch and listening to her rhythmic breathing as she falls asleep.

My thoughts about her body are under control, and I can't help but think about how nice it is. I lean back against the cushions, sleep threatening to take me under as Lennon pushes closer, and I can't help but soak up the contact.

My thumb strokes her shoulder on impulse, and I close my eyes.

Lennon and I are friends.

And I don't mind that at all.

· · · ● · ● · ● · · ·

The alarm on my phone rouses me, and I wake up wrapped around a warm body on my couch. The couch in my home where I live.

Oh shit.

I slowly peel myself away from her, untangle our legs, and carefully grab my device from the ottoman to shut off the alarm.

Lennon stirs, and I freeze. How am I supposed to play this off? We didn't have sex, but somehow, what we did feels like more.

Friendship. That's what I was thinking before I fell asleep, but I've never woken up tangled with Griffin or Ryan.

Fuck.

I stand up, noting the new text message that came through from *Morgan from the Conference*, but I ignore it. I have class this morning and need to make sure I'm ready to leave by eight.

"Hey." Lennon sits up, her arms stretching overhead and revealing a flash of skin that I don't need to be seeing.

Act casual.

"Hey," I say, tugging at the hood of my sweatshirt. "I have class this morning, and I'm going to make some coffee. You're welcome to–" *What am I even saying?* "Hang around, I guess. Do you take cream in your coffee?"

"Cream and sugar," she says, a soft smile kissing her lips. "Thanks."

Lennon stands and folds the flannel blanket we shared last night, tossing it over one side of the sectional. She's not acknowledging anything. She's not bringing up the kiss, talking about how we fell asleep. I'm starting to wonder what she's thinking–what's in her head.

"You don't have to do that," I say, discomfort making my stomach churn.

"It's no problem," she answers. "I need to get going soon, anyway. I'll have to call someone about the chimney situation. I don't think the bats are so scary in the daytime."

She's so relaxed–so comfortable that I question my own sanity. Maybe it didn't mean anything to her. She's certainly acting like it meant nothing as she grabs her bag from by the door and digs in for a toothbrush and toothpaste.

It didn't mean anything. She said that after I kissed her, and maybe she actually meant it.

"You think they'll get out to look at the chimney today?" I ask.

If I'm being honest, Lennon didn't *do* anything last night that would make me think she wanted more from me. She's just here–hanging out–and despite my reaction, I still liked having her here last night.

"Probably not." She stands. "It's no big deal, though." She smiles as I shove my hands into my sweatshirt pocket. "I'll just close my bedroom door at night."

"Well, let me know if you need anything." I walk toward the kitchen, dragging my feet. "The chimney is off the table, but I'm sure I could help some more with the Inn."

"No need," she says, and I can't help but question my disappointment at those two words. "Bonfire next weekend?"

I turn to look at her, offering a smile of my own. "Sure. I'll be there."

Eleven

Lennon

I've spent the better part of two days looking through paper-work, researching, and trying to set a timeline for when the bed-and-breakfast will open. I haven't quit my job at the pediatric office, but I saved up some time to take while I was getting moved in and planning what came next. Renovating on a budget will be a challenge, but I'm sure I can find some thrifted pieces to help make the space look the way I've always dreamed about.

For now, I've decided not to stress about it. The place came with charm already, so there's no point in worrying.

I tug on the door to the red barn behind the house, pulling until it slides open, revealing the dusty remnants of the previous tenants' homesteading addiction. I heard they had chickens and a few goats–something that may be fun to bring back in, eventually.

In the meantime, I decide to check out the vintage bike I found when I was touring the place. Hopefully, it's still tucked at the back of the barn on the ground floor beneath the hayloft, where a few bales from the previous owners remain. For the most part, the barn was used for storage, but the bike was relatively new.

I guess they didn't want to take it with them.

I smile when I see the bike leaning against the wall exactly where it was before–in perfect condition. I'm meant to get coffee with Cass in an hour since she took today off–presumably to get an explanation of my frantic Facetime call three days ago.

I tug the handlebars and walk the bike into the light to give my assessment. The weather has shifted to second summer, apparently, and I've never been more pissed at the inconsistency of Ohio weather in September. I was hoping for sweaters and boots, not vintage jeans and a white crop top. The jeans happen to be my protest against the eighty-degree temperatures. It kind of ruins the fall vibe.

The tires look decent, and I test it out, deciding to shove the thing into the back of my car so I can go for a ride near the coffee shop–autumn dreams and trying to force the colder weather again.

More importantly, as I close the car door and get in the front seat, I'm trying not to think about last weekend, but I list off what happened, anyway.

Noah kissed me.

He told me we were just friends.

He watched movies with me all night.

And then I woke up with his raging hard-on pressed against my ass before continuing the morning by pretending it never happened.

My brows furrow when I pull into the parking lot and stop the car. I've never been more confused by a man's behavior. And when I was testing out every dating app on the market earlier this year, I gained quite a bit of experience, so I would know.

Noah was very clear about his intentions of friendship, so I'm not really thinking, *what does this mean?* It means nothing and the chances that the kiss meant something to him?

Unlikely.

Plus, I don't even like him. Or didn't, rather.

I hop on the bike, circling the block a few times before parking it by the coffee shop door and heading inside. The familiar sounds and smells welcome me in as I spot Cass sitting at one of the small tables by the window. Her perfectly styled blonde hair hangs around her shoulders, and unlike me, Cass has fully dressed for the heat as if autumn didn't exist. Between the sunglasses, the fitted brown tank, high-waisted white shorts, and accessories, she looks expensive.

I sometimes forget how Ellis and Cass met. It seems like she's been a part of our friend group forever, and while I know Cass dated some insufferable rich man, I have trouble imagining it.

Being a weekday, the coffee shop feels nearly empty. I stand next to Cass's table, smiling. "Long time no see," I say, trying like hell to pretend I don't have anything to fill her in on.

"Get your coffee, and then I need you to explain to me why you were at Noah's." For Cass, her tone is far too demanding. She's usually the bubbly one–the sweet one.

"Damn, okay. What has gotten into you?" I ask.

She leans back, crossing her legs beneath the wooden table as she grips her coffee with ringed fingers. "I'm desperate for some kind of gossip. I've been working my ass off at the bar. Since you bought a house, I'm thinking about doing the same thing." She waves a hand to shoo me away. "Now go."

I order my chai latte and make my way back to the table, throwing my cross-body bag onto one of the extra chairs and sliding into position.

"So," Cass begins, a wide smile on her face. "Noah?"

I laugh, suddenly embarrassed because here I am, explaining something I don't fully understand myself. He's so hot and cold. "It's a long story," I say.

Cass leans in, pulling her blonde strands of hair over one shoulder and acting as if we are about to share some kind of secret. She's not wrong–maybe.

"Good thing I took today off," she says.

I fill her in on the toilet, the bat, the ER, the kiss, the movie, the odd wake-up, and the way I haven't heard from Noah since Sunday. And the whole time, Cass's mouth hangs open as if every new revelation is a shock to her.

"Why the fuck are you looking at me like that?" I ask, eyes narrowed.

"No reason." She brings her coffee to her lips, taking a sip and looking away as if she knows some secret.

I grimace. "It's nothing. Noah doesn't do relationships. I'm starting to think the man maintains about a million situationships at one time."

Her blue eyes snap to mine. "And you've become one of them."

"Like hell I have!" Or maybe I have; I'm not sure. "It's not like I slept with him. Besides, the kiss was a one-time thing."

Cass taps a red nail on the table's wooden surface. The bell on the door rings as another customer walks in. "Remember that book you gave me last week? The really smutty one with the–"

"This is real life," I say, knowing exactly where she's going with this. I recall the book.

Mostly.

"Listen," I start. "He has a great ass. He kisses like it's an Olympic sport, and he happens to hold every gold medal ever. I'm attracted to him, but that's temporary. We are *friends*." Somehow, I don't think she is convinced.

"Exactly. All I was saying," she says, rolling her eyes. "Maybe you two *should* sleep together. Get some of the tension out of the way and–"

She stops talking abruptly, blue eyes going wide as they catch something by the front door.

"What?" I say before turning to find our topic of conversation strolling into the very same coffee shop and wearing one of his infamous pairs of slacks with a white button down. The sleeves are rolled to his elbows, and honestly, it's kind of rude for him to be such a walking fucking thirst trap.

God. What was she saying about sleeping with him? I haven't gone on a date since the fucker at the art show. The summer has been busy planning for this home purchase. A real dry spell.

"What a coincidence," Cass says, a smile pulling at her mouth.

I watch Noah stride to the counter and blatantly flirt with the woman taking his order. He's leaning toward her, throwing a wink in her direction and turning up the charm. Insufferable, actually. I can't believe I had been warming up to him all weekend. He's easy to like but definitely not someone to get involved with seriously.

I turn away.

Clearly, he didn't see us.

Or did he?

I pretend it doesn't feel like lead in my stomach. "Anyway," I start. I slide my finger around the top of my coffee cup. "You're taking extra hours at the bar to buy a house?"

Cass jumps at the conversation, explaining that she's been feeling off since last year when her boyfriend cheated on her–thinking that it's time to try something new.

"Hey."

My eyes flick up and lock with Noah's, not sure how to gauge this interaction.

I'm being fucking stupid thinking about it. Noah established that we are friends. We are *friends.*

I should stop pretending I didn't enjoy his company. I did. I also enjoyed his tongue down my throat—an unfortunate complication, really.

I should just act exactly how I would in any other situation. Talk to him as if nothing happened.

"Hey, asshat." *Friendly.*

One side of his mouth quirks up before he acknowledges Cass. "Hey, Cass."

"Hi," she squeaks.

I lean back, taking a long drag of coffee and hoping that Noah will fill the silence for me. I've never had trouble filling silence before.

"Got any more projects you need help with?" he asks.

I relax into my seat, setting my coffee on the table and chuckling. "Are you trying to befriend another bat?" I say, cocking an eyebrow in his direction.

The smile dances on his lips. "Possibly."

When I look at Cass, I catch the curious expression on her face—the one that says she is thinking about something devious—something I don't need to hear.

"So," I say, trying to distract from Cass's expression. "You're coming to the bonfire this Saturday?"

Noah's hand flexes around his cup of coffee. "Yes," he answers.

We stare at each other. The silence that stretches between us feels loaded with memories of every interaction from this past weekend—every touch that was the very opposite of what *friends* would take part in. I think Noah feels it, too.

"I *do* have more projects if you're interested." I'm distracting from the obvious tension. For some reason, I can't get enough of him. I'm coming to terms with the fact that there can't be anything other than a casual relationship with Noah, but maybe Cass is right. We could get it out of our systems and then part ways. It would help the charged undertones.

"Is that so?" he says before rolling his tongue along his cheek. "What will I be learning to do this time?"

There's a number of projects I could give him, so it's easy to figure one out. "The porch could use some work."

"At this point, I'm thinking I'll just learn to build a house from the ground up. Tear down your little bed-and-breakfast in the making and build you a mansion instead."

My stomach flips, which is exactly the opposite of what it should be doing, so I don't acknowledge it. "Wow," I say. "You find me repulsive, but for some reason, you're willing to build me a whole mansion."

His brow furrows. "I don't find you repulsive, Lennon."

Clearly. It would be hard to kiss the way he did if he thought so. My cheeks heat, and I'm all too aware of Cass's eyes on us. She knows about the kiss. I suddenly feel like the word *horny* is tattooed on my head, and I'm embarrassed.

She clears her throat, and I'm forced to glance her way. By the look on her face, she's plotting. I just know it.

Noah clears his throat, drawing my attention back to his brown eyes and the veins of his forearms taunting me in a way that is so female gaze I might pass out.

He shifts on his feet. "Text me what it is you're wanting done. I'll try to find some time between classes tomorrow."

When he turns, heading out the glass doors and leaving me in the presence of Ohio's most cut-throat detective, apparently.

"Okay," Cass says, breaking the silence. "So, what's *actually* going on?"

I lean back, casting my gaze up toward the ceiling as I sigh. "Fuck if I know, dude. Fuck if I know."

Twelve

Noah

My last class ended in the early afternoon, followed by my office hours, where I had at least three students come in to ask ridiculous questions about the assignment due next week. Unfortunately, I couldn't bring myself to focus on anything other than seeing Lennon again. So, I found myself more irritable than usual when explaining, for the third time, what a rhetorical analysis paper consists of.

As I leave my office, the sun sits low on the horizon, bright pinks and purples streaking across the clear autumn sky. Checking my watch, I wince. I'm positive I'm going to be late for dinner with my parents.

It's been a few weeks since I've had time, and my mother has taken to calling me three times a day for the last two days to ensure that I plan to keep my promise and show up after work. I'm not sure why she's worried. I always show up when they invite me.

Climbing into my black Honda, I toss my leather bag into the passenger seat, put the key in the ignition, and promptly grab my phone from my pocket.

I haven't heard from Lennon since I left the coffee shop this morning, and the anticipation is eating away at my resolve. I have to text her.

> **Me:** You said something about the porch?

I stare at the device, waiting for a response. A solid two minutes go by before I decide I can't risk being any later than I already am, but when the three dots pop up on the screen, indicating that she's typing, I stay put. My willingness to negotiate my priorities feels problematic—a sort of litmus test for how the woman has slowly burrowed her way beneath my skin. My mind is now hyper-aware of her existence, and it feels as if there's no going back.

A photo of the porch comes through.

> **Lennon:** The railing is loose, and I'm pretty sure there's a board that needs replaced. Might need more. Think it's manageable?

The photo displays the wrap-around porch that I walked on the two other times I went to her house. Three times, if I count stopping by to pick up her things before she stayed over. I'm no expert, clearly, but I'm pretty sure the porch needs more than a sturdier railing and a few new pieces of wood. It would be a time commitment to learn how to fix all the issues that thing had.

Me: I can figure it out.

I leave the college, counting down the minutes from work to my parents' house, and try to convince myself I'm not bothered by Lennon's strange behavior earlier.

She acted so casually at the coffee shop this morning. While we are friendlier than before, you wouldn't have been able to tell that we spent all night on my couch by the conversation we were having. You wouldn't know that she's one of the few people close to me who knows about Alexis aside from my family or that I am now privy to the small glimpse of her dynamic with her father.

I know how she tastes, the kinds of movies she likes, the way her breath feels on my lips–

It's the kind of intimacy I avoid strategically, but Lennon appears unaffected. There's no end goal there, but then why would there be an end goal?

The damage has been done. Things are complicated.

With the sun sinking lower, the light dims further, leaves floating along the wind outside the car. I clench the steering wheel harder, my knuckles turning white.

It was one hell of a kiss, and as far as I can tell, it meant absolutely nothing to her. Somehow, that is exactly the type of situation I look for, but this is *Lennon*.

This whole thing began because I felt I had something to prove. I wanted to prove that I was capable of more than my reputation. When I picked that fight last spring, I knew I was doing the right thing. As soon as Griffin started hanging out with Ellis, I knew things were serious. Things *are* serious. And Lennon comes as a package deal.

I didn't want her to be hurt. I thought I could help and protect those in the new circle of friends I'd formed since Alexis. Deep down, I'd also wanted Lennon to *like* me. Especially since Lennon didn't seem to like anyone.

And now, I'm realizing how difficult it is to earn her approval. I'm not sure why the fuck I want it so badly.

When I pull into my parents' driveway, I throw the car into park and quickly snatch my phone from the passenger seat. Finding another text from her, I roll my shoulders in a feeble attempt to rid my body of frustration, and looking at her message does just that.

Her response feels like that approval I'd been seeking.

Lennon: You know, I could download a dating app again. I'm sure someone would be willing to fix all this shit. Then I wouldn't bother you.

My brows furrow as I type my response.

Why the fuck would she think she's bothering me? I'm practically begging for her attention, anyway.

Me: You're not bothering me.

Me: Also. You're on dating apps?

It shouldn't come as a shock that a single woman in her mid-twenties would be using dating apps, but it makes me wonder how many dates she's been on since last spring. She said she would have to download the app again, so she's clearly not using it currently. Maybe she deleted it because she *is* dating someone.

No, that wouldn't make sense. Lennon wouldn't have kissed me if she were dating someone else.

Then again, there's the chance that she's in a casual relationship—one where they're welcome to see other people. In which case, kissing me would be fully on the table.

I wince, my gut churning at the thought of Lennon with someone else—anyone else.

I'm not sure they'd be good enough for her.

What kind of man is she even looking for?

Her newest text comes through.

> **Lennon:** How do you think I met your ex's little friend?

I snort.

> **Me:** Makes sense. Do you like using dating apps?

Fuck, I sound stupid.

> **Lennon:** Planning on getting your own account, Noah?

> **Lennon:** Wait, do you already have one?

> **Me:** I don't.

I hesitate, fully aware that the message now sitting and waiting to be sent puts us in different territory. Asking seems like going too far, and still, I can't help but wonder how she will answer.

The firm tapping sound on my car window startles me as I look up to see my dad waiting there, dragging the trash behind him.

I pocket my phone and get out of the vehicle to be met with my father's deep scowl. The wrinkles carve themselves deeper into the center of his forehead with his disappointment, bushy eyebrows lowered in a way that reminds me of my childhood.

Equal parts kind and firm, my father had always believed in no nonsense. That is unless he donned those false Halloween teeth and a strange wig for the sheer joy of vacuuming up stink bugs while making my mother laugh. He'd always had a way of committing to the bit, calling himself an exterminator and bringing an infectious joy to what would arguably be a disgusting infestation of common midwestern pests.

Though his wrinkles are deeper, and I find myself noting all the physical changes that come with parents aging, he's still the same dad. Especially when he's scolding me.

"I'm just taking the garbage down, but your mom's waiting, Son. Get off your damn phone."

He hardly acknowledges me as he pulls the can down to the curb, and I close the door behind me, feeling somewhat like a child.

"You realize I'm over thirty, Dad."

He makes his way back up the gently sloped driveway, a pale hand running along his graying beard. "Not around here, you're not." He places a hand on my shoulder, just shy of too firm, as he directs me to the door. It's only when he squeezes a touch that the smile breaks on his face. "Missed you this week," he says.

"Missed you guys, too."

The front door swings open, and I'm greeted with warm air and fond memories as I hang my coat in the closet. The stairs to the right still have a long gallery of my school photos leading the way and making me wish I'd had a sibling so the whole thing would look less like a shrine.

My dad disappears down the hall, headed toward the kitchen at the back of the house as I check my phone again on impulse–eager for any scrap of attention from Lennon.

Lennon: What do I look for in guys, you mean?

Me: Yeah, I guess.

I quickly tuck my phone in my pocket again to ward off the embarrassment of the question I'm asking. Lennon comes with a brazenness that I find attractive. She's outspoken, true to herself, loyal, and clearly devoted to whatever it is she wants to do. Alexis was the exact inverse of that. Directionless, certainly not loyal, and nowhere near as outspoken. It's probably why there were so many secrets she was hiding from me.

With Lennon, it's different. She's honest to the point of being rude, but something about that relaxes me. I don't have to worry about how she's perceiving me. It's like that brazenness gives me permission to reveal my true self.

Being friends with Lennon is easy.

Aside from how convoluted our friendship has gotten.

I find my family in the kitchen, my mom chopping vegetables as my dad sorts through mail by the kitchen table, presumably working towards clearing it off for our dinner.

"There's my son," my mom says, her eyes focused on the mutilated carrot before her. "I was beginning to think you did not exist. I thought that maybe you were a ghost."

I chuckle, wrapping an arm around her and kissing her on the side of the head. Her warmth seeping into me despite her attitude about me missing last week's dinner.

"It's so good to see you too, Mom. I'm so glad I'm not like any of those other adult children that move states away from their parents and never call."

She lets out a *humph* and continues working.

When my phone vibrates, I'm drawn to it like a moth to a flame.

I grab a glass from the cabinet, using the filter on the refrigerator to fill it and take a sip as I check my newest message.

Lennon: I typically look for large penises.

I choke on my drink, my dad coming around to pat my back and ask me if I've ever had water before.

"I'm fine," I mutter, setting the glass down on the counter.

Me: The most important of qualities, I'm sure. Is that your conversation starter? A request for dick pics?

Once again, her response is almost immediate. I feel as though I've won the lottery with the rapid reply.

> **Lennon:** Oh, absolutely. I have to fully assess the situation before anyone is allowed any physical contact.

I can't fight the smirk tugging at the corner of my mouth.

> **Me:** You've gotten lax with your requirements. I got to kiss you without the proper vetting.

> **Lennon:** I thought we weren't talking about that.

> **Me:** We aren't.

> **Lennon:** You brought it up.

> **Me:** I did.

And I'm not sure why. After my long speech about regretting the kiss, I'm drawing even more attention to it. Maybe it's because I don't actually regret it.

That kiss has imprinted itself on my mouth and in my memory—the soft strands of her hair, the way her body melted into mine, the feel of her plump lips.

"Noah," my mom's voice snaps me out of my thoughts. "Here," she says, passing a cucumber, a small wooden cutting board, and a knife to me. "If you're here, help. Cut this, please. Besides, it will be good for you."

I chuckle. "Of course, Mom."

Lennon: Would you like me to judge yours? I'm happy to rate your penis, Noah.

I can feel my heart beating like a kick drum in my chest. I stand in front of the cutting board, gripping the cucumber in my hand and snapping a photo, quickly sending it to Lennon before getting to work.

The kitchen is relatively quiet as my dad stands next to my mom, planting a kiss on her temple and looking so in love. It makes me question the last five years of my life.

I was so close to emulating that kind of relationship–or so I thought.

For the longest time, my parents' quiet and steady affection was my most formative example of love. It was something I grew to crave. So, when Alexis and I began getting serious, I jumped at the chance to create a marriage like theirs.

The only problem is my parents have lasted decades, and my relationship fell apart so quickly it was almost embarrassing.

It's hard to believe how experiences can change your perspective on love. One bad memory can poison the concept forever.

I cut the cucumber, talking to my mom about her newest obsession with adult paint by numbers kits. June Peterson, Griffin's mom, is a well-known local artist. She is also one of my mom's best friends.

My mom continues cooking while speaking. "It makes me feel as if I could be as good as her, you know?"

I smile, stealing a piece of carrot from the salad she's prepared and popping it in my mouth. "June cannot cook, Mother. You don't have to be as good at painting. You have your own talents."

My mom looks up, dark eyes blazing. "I'll have whatever talents I would like to have, Noah."

I chuckle again, and so does my dad as he wraps a hand around her waist. "Of course, sweetie. You are the most talented."

"Go set the dining room table, Noah. We are about ready to eat," she says, and I use the opportunity to check my phone once more.

Lennon: A ten for size, but I'm taking points off for the green coloring. An eight out of ten isn't so bad.

Me: Does that mean I passed?

I'm smiling wider, setting plates around the kitchen table as my mom brings the food in.

Lennon: You coming to fix the porch tomorrow?

I type out one last message, promising that I'm going to soak up some time with my family.

Me: Of course, I'll be there tomorrow. No classes until evening. I can be there in the morning.

Lennon: Nine in the morning is good.

Me: Yeah, okay. Nine is good.

Thirteen

Lennon

"So, it may need a little more than one new board. Also, nice pants."

Noah chuckles and shoves his hands into the black jeans he's wearing, kicking up rocks from the gravel driveway as we make our way to the base of the steps. He shoved the sleeves of his dark green henley to his elbows, revealing the veins running along his forearms.

Definitely something I don't need to be seeing.

It's indecent.

"No shit," he says. Stopping and turning next to me. "I've been here three times, Lennon. I knew this would be more work than you were saying."

"Is that why you're wearing jeans?" I ask. "I've never seen you wear jeans."

He smiles, white teeth flashing. "So, you like them? I knew they made my ass look good."

I can't fight the smirk that sneaks onto my face as I roll my eyes. He's certainly not wrong, but I refuse to acknowledge the arrogance of that statement. "So, can you fix it?"

Noah leans in, crowding my space just enough that my pulse quickens. His voice is lower, making his next statement feel almost intimate. It's too much this early in the morning.

For a casual friendship, my ovaries sure love to scream at me in his presence.

"Of course, I can fix it, Lennon."

Jesus Christ.

I clear my throat, anxious to place a little distance between us—anything to break apart some of the tension. He had said that one kiss was all I'd get, so I don't know why he is here or why I feel like this.

Maybe I'm just a terrible friend.

"I'm planning on putting a gallery wall up in the living room while you work on this, but I already bought the treated wood. It's in there." I nod towards the red barn, but Noah's gaze stays firmly fixed on mine, a small smile permanently etched into his features.

"You never answered my question," he says, and I frown.

"What question?"

"Did I pass?" He rolls his tongue along his cheek, but I'm still not fully registering what he's talking about.

I shake my head, scoffing. "Pass high school algebra? What do you mean?"

Noah laughs again, taking another step forward until his forearm rests against the wooden plank connecting the porch to the porch's cover. I hadn't realized I backed up, and now, with him this close, it feels like there's no air left to fill up my lungs. "Please," he says, and my eyes flick down toward his lips just as his tongue darts out to wet them. "I sent you the best dick pic I had, and you didn't even tell me if I passed?"

The cucumber.

My stomach flips when he continues holding my gaze. "You said we wouldn't be kissing again," I say, my voice barely audible. "What would be the point of giving you a passing score?"

When he speaks, I can almost feel the vibrations on my skin. "What if I said I can't stop thinking about it?" he says. "What if I wanted to do it again?"

My chest is rising and falling rapidly with every shallow breath.

Maybe Cass had a point. Maybe there is something here, and we need to just get it out of our systems. I certainly wouldn't mind, but it would be imperative that I keep my head on straight—establish exactly what we would be doing as to not spook him.

"Why wouldn't you kiss me?" I ask. "The first time I brought it up."

Noah leans back a bit, shock plainly written on his face.

I'd love to say it didn't bother me–love to say that I am perfectly fine not knowing, but that wouldn't be true. I want to know what was in his head then and why it suddenly changed. If I'm going to ask for what I want, we need to have some clear communication first.

"I–" he pauses, gathering himself. "I don't know," he admits. "I wanted to, but we have mutual friends. I thought it would complicate things."

My nose crinkles at the thought. Sure, kissing Noah could come with complications–it *has* come with complications–but the man's an expert in casual. To some extent, he shouldn't fear complications. "So, you eventually decided that didn't matter and kissed me anyway?"

Noah looks almost offended. "Well, we spent an entire night on the couch after. We were watching movies. You didn't act like anything changed. You called me an asshat three days later."

"A term of endearment, I promise." I'm not sure why I'm pressing. I know who he is–or at least what his reputation is. Maybe I just want to be clearer about what's going on before I jump into whatever this is. If I can assure him there are no complications and assert that I know exactly what *this* is, maybe he will feel comfortable enough to give in to whatever desire he's confessing. "I'm not under the false impression that you want anything more from me than sex."

"That's not true."

I gawk at him. "It's not?"

"We're friends. At least, I'd like to be." Noah still looks somewhat offended, and I decide that I'm going to do something very, very stupid.

I press one last time. "Friends that kissed."

"I guess."

This porch may never get fucking fixed and at this point I'm okay with that. At least the chimney guy did his part, and I don't have to worry about bats anymore.

"Okay," I start, trying to keep my tone level. "Why don't we just have sex?"

That got him. *Good*.

Noah looks like I've grown three heads and started speaking French.

He's already rejected me once, so there's no point in being fearful of that. The worst he can do is say no, though I'm really hoping that won't be the case.

"Just once," I say. "We can deal with whatever this weird tension is, get it out of our systems, and carry on exactly as you say. We can be friends."

His face looks blank, and I can't for the life of me figure out what he's feeling. He's probably going to say no. Again.

"Why?" he asks.

I turn, taking one step up the stairs to get away from him. I've been more than clear–done everything I can to prove to him that I won't come crawling and begging for a committed relationship–assuming that's what he's so afraid of.

Why? Because he's hot? Because, for some strange reason, I trust him? Because I must be in the worst dry spell ever with how badly I want to feel his hands on me.

I scoff, moving back down the steps to stand directly in front of him. "Because I want to have sex with you, Noah."

"You're sure?" he asks, and I roll my eyes.

"Yes I'm fucking sure. I wouldn't have asked if I weren't–"

His mouth is on mine before I can get another word out, hungry and seeking as he grips my face in his hands, desperate to draw me closer.

The soft press of his lips, the warmth of his skin, all of it has my stomach flipping, my breath catching as if he's stolen it completely. His fingers are in my hair, tangling in the red strands as I grip his shirt, pulling until he presses his body against mine, backing me into the railing he's supposed to be fixing.

I pray to all the gods it doesn't fucking break.

"Is that a yes?" I whisper, our breaths mingling. He tastes like espresso, and I briefly consider changing my coffee order from chai to whatever he drinks in the morning.

Without responding, he's kissing me again, teeth tugging at my bottom lip as if he's trying to devour me. When his tongue runs along the seam of my lips, requesting access, I moan, desperate for more.

Noah's hands move from my face to my hips, slowly migrating toward my ass before he picks me up, allowing me to feel how fucking hard he is.

He pulls back, lips hovering over mine, eyes searching. "Where?" he asks.

I suck in a breath–another–forcing the direction from my lips. Honestly, I'd have zero complaints about him fucking me against the railing. "Bedroom's on the ground floor," I answer, "just off the kitchen." A small sound squeaks out when he squeezes my ass in his firm grip, turning to step up onto the porch. "Don't fucking drop me. You still haven't fixed this."

Noah chuckles, his mouth back on mine as he carries me through the house, the screen door slamming behind us until he sets me on my feet in the bedroom.

My hands are gripping the bottom of his shirt, tugging upward until it's off, and I get the view of him shirtless in my room, turned on and looking at me as if I'm the only thing he's ever wanted.

Noah's hand sneaks under my shirt, his thumb flicking out over my nipple and sending a jolt of pleasure through my body. I tip my head back, his lips on my neck, hands working until the shirt is gone, his fingers unhooking my belt before tugging my jeans off.

When he steps back, his dark gaze takes in the black lace thong, my lips part.

Noah climbs onto the bed, pushing the comforter back and lying directly in the center.

"Get up here," he says, and I listen. Straddling his legs and wondering why he's still wearing pants at all.

I press down, grinding myself against him to get some kind of relief before his fingers tuck into the sides of my underwear, and he gently pulls down. I move until they're completely off, and there's no hiding how wet I am.

He grabs my ass, pulling me up his body, and I freeze. When he catches my hesitation, I tilt my head to the side, my hair spilling in a curtain around us.

"What?" I ask, and he smirks, the expression leaving me wanting more.

Noah keeps his hands firmly planted and tugs again. "I want you to sit on my face, Lennon."

Holy shit.

"Are you–"

He chuckles again, and I can feel the sound everywhere. "I'm sure," he says. "Now, come on and get up here."

My pulse spikes, nerves slowly leaking in. I've never done this before, but I don't hesitate. I crawl up until I'm hovering over him, my knees on either side of his head. Noah lets out a dark sound from deep in his throat, one that has me desperate with need.

"Put your hands on the headboard," he commands, and I oblige just before his arms wrap around me, hands pulling my waist down until I can feel his tongue right where I need him most.

"Oh shit." My hands grip the headboard, knuckles turning white as I suck in a breath through my teeth. I've never felt this out of control. With every lick, I'm fighting the urge to move my hips, trying to hold myself up enough so he can breathe. The sensation builds, and I know I'm not going to last long.

My entire body is lit aflame when Noah tugs me down more, another sound rumbling from deep in his throat. He keeps working me as if he's a starved man, and I have the pleasure of providing him with his last meal on earth.

With his fingers digging into my thighs, I give in, allowing myself to give chase to the promise of an orgasm I know is within reach.

"Noah," I pant, moving my hips. He encourages me with another deep sound. "I can't. I'm–"

His grip tightens, and with one final drag of his tongue, I'm shuttering around him, barely holding myself up.

When the pleasure slowly fades, leaving me boneless, he grabs my waist. Guiding me down his body, I follow his lead until my hands are on his chest, and I can feel his cock straining in his jeans.

I tug at his belt as he watches me work his pants down until he's fully naked in my bed.

My mind misfires as I take him in, fully on display and sprawled out. I cannot believe I'm having sex with Noah Ashwood.

He sits up, my knees on either side of his hips, as he reaches into the pocket of his jeans that are now tossed to the side on the mattress. He opens his wallet, fishes out a condom, and grips it in his hand as he captures my mouth in a smoldering kiss.

My entire body burns with the heat of his lips. A flush blooms over my face, down my neck, and across my chest. When I look down at Noah as he pulls back, his lips are swollen, eyes hooded with desire.

"I haven't been able to stop thinking about this since you demanded I kiss you." He moves my hair off my shoulder, fingers slowly ghosting the skin, sending electricity everywhere.

"Yeah?" I breathe, my fingers exploring the planes of his chest.

"Yeah," he confirms before bringing the condom up and tearing the wrapper with his teeth.

When he's fully sheathed, I line myself up over him, feeling the press of his cock against my entrance as I slowly sink down.

A whimper escapes past my lips as he stretches me slowly until he's filling me completely.

His mouth presses against my neck, drawing out sounds until I'm moving, grinding against him in a way that has me climbing all over again.

I've been on a lot of dates. Had a handful of serious relationships, but I've never had sex like *this*. I can't help but wonder what that means—if one time will be enough.

Noah's hands find my hips again, encouraging me to press down harder—faster.

"You feel so good, Lennon." His voice is low, as if he's sharing an intimate secret. "That's it," he says. "Take what you need."

My eyes close, hair softly brushing against my back as I move, listening to Noah's breath in my ear. It's all too much—building until I can't take it anymore.

The pleasure peaks, my body slowing, riding out the last of the aftershocks until I'm sated.

Noah smirks, one arm looping under my ass and flipping us over until he's on top, thrusting and looking like a God as he hovers over me.

My eyes trace the lines of his face, his arms, his chest—soaking in every inch of him as he moves, his hair mussed with a strand falling across his brow. There's a sheen of sweat coating every inch of skin, and when I lean forward, kissing his collarbone, my tongue flicks out to taste him.

It's salt and movie nights on the couch. I can't seem to get enough of him.

I lie back, and Noah gently grabs my wrists, pinning them overhead.

"Look at you," he says, his eyes drinking me in. "Fuck, Lennon. You're taking me so well."

He sits up, his hands moving from my wrists to grip the sides of my waist as he pulls me to him. At this angle, he's so *deep* I can hardly think.

That's when I feel it. "Oh my God," I whisper, the slow build starting again.

Noah's face is determined as he gently slides one hand over my stomach, down until his fingers press right where I need him. He's moving, rubbing, climbing with me as I arch upward.

When his thrusts turn more erratic, low sounds escaping his throat, I close my eyes, feeling everything as we both finish together.

Noah leans down, gently kissing me before he rolls off, leaving us both sweaty and panting.

"That was–" I don't finish the sentence.

"Yeah," he breathes.

I try to soak it up–keep any thoughts at bay as I recover. He's ruined me for everyone else, and the worst part is we only get once.

What a fucking mess.

"So–" I start, not sure how to respond. Noah's used to this kind of thing. He does this a lot. I let out a breathy chuckle, trying not to show how I'm feeling. "This is the part where you leave?" I ask.

Noah laughs, leaning over and threading his arm between my legs, his hand on my back as he lifts me up and flips me over. My head rests on his chest, one leg thrown over his.

"I can't leave, yet," he whispers, his hand running over my hair. "Let's just lay here for a minute." He kisses the top of my head. "Then I can fix your porch."

I nestle even closer, soaking up the scent of his cologne–vanilla and tobacco with a hint of espresso. My eyes grow heavy, my body sated and molded to his as sleep finally pulls me under.

Fourteen

Noah

Sweat drips down my back when I finally return the saw and sander to the barn by Lennon's house. Somehow, the late-afternoon sun beats down on me, making everything unbearably hot. Tall trees surround the bed-and-breakfast, but the treeline sits far enough away that it does nothing to shade the porch or the yard between the house and the barn.

At a balmy seventy degrees, the temperature isn't actually unpleasant. I think I've just been working too hard–trying to expel some of the energy I still can't seem to shake. Sleeping with Lennon should have left me sated and ready to move on. In fact, that had been the offer. Sleep together. Move on.

So, when we'd finally crawled out of bed, I set to fixing the porch with renewed fervor if only to keep myself from crawling to her, begging her for one more taste.

Sex with Lennon is–

Over. It's not happening again, and everything about that arrangement is pissing me off. I've been cutting wood, nailing boards in place, sanding the porch down, sealing everything appropriately. It doesn't matter how much manual labor I do, I can't seem to stop thinking about every harsh breath–every sound I pulled from between those plump lips.

It certainly wasn't enough. I've had plenty of sex–nothing like that.

The screen door of the house bangs shut when I get back to the porch, eyes catching Lennon's where she stands at the top of the steps, her arms folded across her chest. A chest I've seen fully.

Fucking hell.

"It looks good," she says, glancing around the porch before testing the railing with her hand. "Sturdy."

I pull the hem of my t-shirt up to wipe the sweat from my face, noting the way Lennon's gaze lingers when I'm done. I'm not sure how to navigate this situation. It feels like I should be free to touch her–kiss her–but again, she was very clear about her intentions.

It was just once.

We were just letting off some steam.

I wipe my hands on my jeans. "How long until this house becomes an actual Inn. Or bed-and-breakfast. I'm not sure I know the difference."

Lennon smiles, leaning against the railing with one foot crossed over the other. "There's a lot of paperwork involved–quite a bit for me to figure out. It's proving to be somewhat of a–" Her face scrunches. "A learning curve. My hope is next summer, but who knows. I'm holding my job at the pediatric office until then."

I tilt my head to the side, noting how much I still don't know about her. "You work in a pediatric office?"

"Yeah." Lennon clears her throat as if she's about to say more, but nothing comes out of her mouth.

"Well," I start. "What do you do there?"

She tugs at a strand of her hair, inspecting the ends. If someone were to watch us, they'd have no idea I had her grinding on my face, my tongue sliding over her clit just hours ago.

"I work the front desk," she says. "It's nothing crazy, but it pays well, and I have benefits, I guess. That's just another thing I'll have to figure out with the bed-and-breakfast." One side of her mouth turns up. "It's not technically an inn since I don't offer a full-blown tavern experience or whatever. The terms are pretty loose, though. At least they are to me."

"You're planning on quitting the job at the pediatric office?"

"Yeah. It served its purpose. Got me this house, but it's not something I want to do long term." She's looking at me now, still leaning against the railing as the sun peeks out to cast her hair in soft light–a true golden hour. "My sister's a doctor, you know?"

"No," I say, holding her gaze. "No, I didn't."

"That's why my father thinks this whole thing is idiotic. Why would I choose to go into hospitality when my older sister went through med school and made something of herself? We have a pretty big age gap. She's thirty-five."

I chuckle. "I'm thirty-two."

Her eyes sparkle as her brows raise. "Geriatric."

Despite her joke, I can tell there's hurt there—not about the age thing, but about her family. I can't imagine how that would feel to have that kind of lack of support. All my parents ever did was provide support. My mom, especially. And even though Lennon seems to be good at hiding her emotions behind a mask, there's still a thread of sadness there.

Last winter, she'd been gone visiting her family. It's why Ellis hired Griffin, anyway. I'm pretty sure she doesn't have family close by, so I assume she's alone in this—being critiqued from a distance.

All the more reason for me to help out.

A few hours ago, I didn't know shit about fixing a porch, and here I am, trying to make the girl who called me an asshat a little less sad.

"Doctorate programs are fucking stupid, anyway. Most of us are in debt, we can't seem to get the stick out of our collective ass, and we firmly believe we are better than everyone else. Doctors are absolute dicks. My piece of paper is impressive, but this," I gesture to the house as a whole. "This is *fun*. It's *difficult*. It takes dedication and hard work to pull something like *this* off, Lennon. It says a lot about you, but we've had some of this conversation before when you were at my house."

She shifts on her feet, uncrossing and then crossing her arms again like I've made her uncomfortable. Maybe I overstepped.

"Do you want to come inside?" she asks. "For some food. I'm sure you're starving."

I glance at the last bit of tools still sprawled out over the deck, deciding that the painting piece can happen later. I have a night class in three hours, but I'm sure I have time to eat. "Sure," I answer, a small smirk forming on my lips.

I stride up the steps, stopping next to her and turning to face her fully. Her eyes flick to my lips–just briefly–and I wonder if she's thinking of the way I felt inside her. I can't seem to stop thinking about it myself. "You're the only one aside from my family that knows about my failed engagement," I admit.

I'm not sure if it's to make her feel more comfortable, or maybe I'm offering a piece of myself in exchange for the piece of her she just gave me.

Lennon scoffs. "I find that hard to believe. I'm sure your friends–"

I raise a brow. "Don't talk to me anymore?" I interrupt. "The friend group I had was all tied up with Alexis. I lost a lot leaving that relationship. I hope she and Hayes are as happy as they deserve."

She fake-gasps, clutching at her heart. "You actually said his name. I thought it was an unspoken rule that we weren't speaking it. Like Voldemort or whatever."

I can't help but crack a smile. "We can nickname him Voldemort if you like. Unless you have another recommendation. You seem to know him better."

"I didn't sleep with him," she says like a confession, and my smile falls. "If that's what you're thinking."

My smile dropped. "I didn't say you did?" There's a question in my tone–the words layered more than I care to admit. I *was* curious, but I wasn't making any assumptions. I sure as hell am not one to talk.

She's staring at me, and somehow, talking about sleeping with people is the furthest from what we should be doing–especially after what happened earlier. I'm not sure how to broach the subject.

"So," I start, dragging out the word. "How are we–" I pause. "Are we acknowledging that–" I'm not sure how to phrase it. "What am I allowed to say about earlier? It was just once, but can I make jokes? Are we talking about it? Are we pretending it never happened?"

"We don't have to talk about it if you don't want to," she says, her voice lower, her expression blank.

I smirk despite the unsettling feeling in my gut. I *want* to talk about it. I *want* to acknowledge it. And worst of all, I want to do it again. "So, I'm your dirty secret, am I?"

She looks away, and I swear her cheeks flush. "Dirty, yes. Secret, no."

God. What is she thinking, and why the fuck does it matter so much?

"Do you want me to order food?" I ask, changing the subject before I say something we'll both regret. "I'm happy to pay for it, but I'll have to leave soon after."

Lennon huffs a laugh, looking incredulous. "You just fixed my entire porch. I'll pay for your fucking meal, Noah."

Rolling her eyes, she pushes off the railing and walks to the door.

Trailing behind her, I rush to catch up, grabbing the handle before she can open it.

Lennon stands in front of me, her eyes wide as I breathe her in. Standing this close sets my skin buzzing like a livewire, my desire potent as I cage her against the door. I want to kiss her again. I want to feel the heat of her skin on mine. I want–

"I'll buy it," I assert, crowding her space and watching as her mouth parts. She pulls in rapid breaths, her chest rising and falling with each drag of air.

Lennon's eyes flick to my lips briefly, and all I can taste is *her*.

I know how it feels to be on the other end of this thing that we've started–wanting simplicity. Admitting that I enjoy spending time with her or showing too much interest may scare her off–though I find it hard to believe Lennon is scared of anything.

She is just now letting me in–letting me *see* her and who she is. I'm clinging to the revelations about her family like a lifeline–too afraid to kiss her again.

I clear my throat, unclasping my hand from the door handle and stepping back.

"Just let me know what you want," I say before pulling my phone from my pocket.

The words feel loaded–and maybe they are. If she asked me to kiss her right now, I would. If she asked anything about Alexis–about my brief spiral thereafter, I may just tell her.

Lennon has me in the palm of her hand, and I don't think she even realizes it.

"I'll order whatever you want," I finally say. "I'm not picky."

Fifteen

Lennon

As it turns out, I'm a fucking idiot.

It is not recent news that I'm impulsive and a bit reckless, but sleeping with Noah was probably the biggest mistake of my adult life. The idea that the attraction would go away if we just went for it one time turned out to be a fallacy–one created from complete delusion.

I'm considering suing Cass for her shit advice. I might as well sue the author of that book as well.

The more time I spend with Noah, the more comfortable I get. It's like hanging out with him is easy–more pleasant than I originally thought possible. And as he sits on the couch across from me in my minimally decorated living room, finishing the sandwich we ordered, I can't help but realize I've made a grave mistake.

I don't want to sleep with Noah just once.

"Okay," I start. "What made you want to get your doctorate?"

I can't get what he said out of my head–the way he was so confident in everything I'm doing. I've spent so much time hearing criticism from my family that I've started ignoring the feelings completely. It doesn't fucking matter what they think because I'm going to do the thing that makes me happy, anyway.

But just because that's true doesn't mean his recognition of my hard work didn't set my dark soul aglow.

Noah smirks in the way that causes a small dimple to appear on his left cheek. I love it.

"I wanted to major in English. It's kind of difficult to do anything with that unless you get a doctorate."

He collects the wrappers off the coffee table and shoves them in the bag before leaning back against the couch. Stretching his arms above his head reveals the small patch of skin he flashed outside earlier when he was wiping the sweat off his forehead. My entire body warms.

"So, you didn't do it just to be an asshole?" I ask, pulling my socked feet up onto the couch and crossing my legs as I face him.

The fireplace crackles from across the room, now fully functioning and making me feel like I'm one step closer to welcoming more stories into the space. I can imagine guests sitting around the fire, sipping hot chocolate while discussing adventures, family–memories. The historic elements of the home charmed me–desperate for more stories to be added. That warm glow of the fire stretches across the floor and kisses the worn wooden coffee table where my e-reader, our trash, and two drinks sit.

Another story the walls of this place will remember.

"No," he says with a laugh. "Despite what you may think, I actually enjoy the teaching aspect."

I raise a brow. "Any excuse to assert that your favorite piece of literature is *Pride and Prejudice* and make the women swoon, I take it?"

He leans forward, placing his elbows on his knees and turning his head sideways to look at me, his hair mussed and his thighs looking criminal in the dirt-streaked jeans he's wearing. "Would you swoon if I said it was *Pride and Prejudice*?"

I scoff, my heart picking up its pace in my chest. "No. Is that really what your favorite classic is?"

He smiles wide, and my stomach flips. "It's not," he says.

I lean forward, fighting the urge to scoot even closer. "Okay, then. What is it, Professor Ashwood? *Wuthering Heights*? Because honestly, I hate that fucking book."

Noah runs a hand through his hair before sitting up and adjusting so he's facing me more fully, one leg propped on the couch.

"I don't hate it, but the characters are objectively insufferable."

I risk touching him–if only because I can't stop myself. I jab his calf with my foot as I speak before pulling it back. "That book deserves more hate. You can hate it, Noah. Nothing brings me more joy than quality time with people who hate the same things I do."

"I'll hate it if that's what it takes to spend more time with you."

My stomach flips as the air in the room disappears–at least that's what it feels like. It's as if the line we could cross is right there, taunting me and begging me to move closer–kiss him again, ask for another round, invite him to stay over.

I finally gather myself. "You never answered my question," I push. "What is it?"

Noah looks embarrassed, rolling his tongue along his teeth before he answers. "*The Scarlet Pimpernel*."

"You're kidding." I laugh as I lean back. "That's quite romantic."

Noah's jaw ticks as if he's holding back a smile. "It's a spy novel."

I lean toward him again, drawn in by his presence as my gaze meets his to make my point. "Noah, he kisses the ground she walks on. It's *romance*."

"Fine," he says. "It has a romantic element to it. What do you read then? You were reading that one day I was over. I bet it's horror novels about chopping up your enemies and burying them in the river."

"I actually just read about people fucking." The look on his face is beyond worth the comment, and I find I very much like pushing the boundaries.

Noah leans around me, snatching the e-reader off the coffee table and turning it on. "You're lying," he says before adding a bookmark to my page and scrolling through the book. I try to grab the device from him, but I'm barely making an effort. It's more of an excuse to get closer, and by the time I give up, our legs are touching.

"No fucking to be seen here, Lennon."

I try to glance at where he's at in the book, unable to figure it out. "It's more of a slow burn," I admit.

He's on a mission, scanning the words across the page and scrolling through until his brows raise as he gets to something good. "Oh, here we go," he says before clearing his throat. "*His hands find their way to my hair, tangling in the brown strands before he tugs gently, baring my neck to him. His mouth is there, hot and seeking as he—*"

"You can stop now," I interrupt. My body warms, remembering the way his hands felt on my waist, demanding and directing as I ground myself on his cock. "You're going to spoil all the fun. I'd like to read it with the appropriate build-up."

"So, it's the build-up for you?" he says, his eyes meeting mine over the screen.

I thumb the fabric of my leggings, my knuckles brushing against his leg and sending a jolt up my arm. "You should know," I say, his eyes darkening. There's a fire there—one I'd be happy to burn in.

"This scene has a lot of dirty talk, too," he starts, his voice lower—taking on a gravel that has heat pooling in my core. "Is that what you like?"

My eyebrow lifts in silent challenge, the fire in my chest growing hotter with every breath. I want to push even more. "I liked when you complimented how I was taking you."

"Yeah?" he says, shifting forward slowly until he's right there—his mouth hovering over mine. "And what about the part when I asked you to sit on my face?"

My breath catches, and I note the way his pupils have blown out, the way it feels like we're wrapped up in some kind of battle—waiting to see who breaks first.

"Maybe," I whisper.

"What if—" His finger traces circles around my knee, slowly moving upward. "What if I told you I liked tasting you. I liked the way it felt when you came on my tongue." His finger moves higher—halfway up my thigh as I finally lose control of my reactions.

My body feels like it's pulled taut and about ready to snap. I'm practically panting when his hand grips the outside of my thigh and squeezes gently.

"Is this enough of a build-up for you, Lennon?" he asks, his bottom lip ghosting over mine. "Or should I drag it out more?"

I suck in a lungful of air, leaning forward and desperate to make contact with his mouth, when a phone alarm blares.

Noah leans back, pulling his phone from his pocket and glancing at the screen. "Shit," he says. "I have to leave now if I'm going to make it in time for my night class."

"Right," I say, clearing my throat before standing up to gather our bag of trash so I can throw it away. I walk across the room, turning back and noting how disheveled he looks, running his hand through his hair, his bicep flexing where the sleeve of his t-shirt ends. "Bonfire tomorrow?"

Noah freezes, eyes meeting mine as a small smile appears on his lips–lips I was so close to kissing again. "Yeah," he says. "Just text me the time."

I nod once before retreating to the kitchen, throwing away our trash and listening as he walks out the door.

My hands grip the scuffed countertops of the kitchen island as I fight to catch my breath.

As I mentioned before, I'm such a fucking idiot.

Sixteen

Noah

The buzzing of the tattoo gun helps empty my mind as I sit in Ryan's shop with Griffin and the few band members from Elephant University, the indie band he currently works for.

Originally, I'd met Griffin at the college where I work. He worked as the video and audio technician before deciding to go on tour. The guy has tattoos covering his body, and Ryan just so happens to be the artist for most of his ink.

The first time I'd met Ryan, I was drunk off my ass after hanging out with Griffin and a few other staff members. Luckily, I made it out without a permanent mark on my body, but a new friend group instead.

What I told Lennon yesterday wasn't a lie. Most of my old friends were tied up with Alexis. I'd been busy in my doctorate program, and so her friends became mine by default. I hadn't had time to put in the effort elsewhere. When we split, most of those people slowly disappeared–fading into the void that is my sad and pathetic past.

"How long are you guys here for?" I ask, tossing a stress ball into the air and catching it.

Ryland looks over at me from the chair as his forearm gets decorated by ink. "We have two shows here, then it's back on the road for a few weeks. We have a long stretch in December, though."

I look at Griffin, who sits across the room with his face in his phone next to one of the other band members. There are five total, I think. Ryland's the lead singer. Then there are others. The only one I remember is the one sitting next to Griffin, and even then, all I know is his name is Nolan, and he plays drums.

"I bet you're happy to be home for Ellis's birthday," I say, and Griffin looks up, one corner of his mouth tugging upwards. "Got any fun plans."

He pockets his phone, shifting and clearing his throat. "About that," he starts, and the sound of the tattoo gun changes as Ryan pulls it away, and everyone glances at Griffin.

"Go on," I encourage, my tone somewhat sarcastic.

"I think I'm going to propose."

The three other guys erupt with congratulations, and all I can think about is the fact that I slept with his future wife's best friend–and he doesn't even know it.

Shit.

I smile because I'm equal parts happy and panicking. Originally, I'd avoided acting on anything with Lennon for fear of complicating things, but it seems that things were destined to be complicated.

Ryan leans back, one gloved hand still holding the tattoo gun, as he runs a brown hand over his face. "You pick a ring yet?" he asks, his grin wide.

"Yeah."

Something in my gut churns at the thought that he's already picked a ring, and this is the first time I'm hearing it. Griffin's been busy, that's for sure. I don't blame him, of course. He has been on the road, and I still have Ryan here. Ryan has his partner, though. Griffin has Ellis, and I have–a whole lot of fucking time on my hands.

"Well," I say, raising my brows. "Let's see it."

Griffin reaches in his pocket and flashes an absolute fucking rock. Somehow, I realize I saw this coming. Griffin's never been the type to date around, and he surely doesn't hook up casually, but even then, I think I knew it was different. Things are different with Ellis. Once they started hanging out, they just didn't stop. It's like he couldn't get enough of her.

I toss the stress ball in the air, a crease forming between my brows. I *am* stressed. Aren't I doing the same thing with Lennon? I've spent an unconscionable amount of time with Lennon—fixing the house, watching her look so natural with Ellis's niece.

In the past month, I've spent more time thinking about the future—the things I had wanted with Alexis that I'd failed so miserably to obtain. The worst part happens to be the small kernel of jealousy in my gut. Guilt overpowers it, but the thing is there, festering and forcing me to realize I might still want... something.

And currently, the only something my mind keeps drawing me back to is Lennon. We are all heading to her house tonight for the bonfire. There's no fucking way I can hide the complications that have come up. I want him to know that it's different—at least for me. It may have been a one-time thing, but Lennon and I are friends.

Well, considering what happened on the couch and the fact that I made out with her last week, we can say it was one and a half times.

Nolan excuses himself to the restroom as Ryan finishes up the tattoo, both of them leaving to check it out in the mirror across the room.

"So, listen," I start, deciding I should just confess—get it over with. "I slept with Lennon."

Griffin blinks, his fingers still curled around the ring box—now frozen. I watch him absorb the information, process, and end on a neutral expression. He nods once. "I figured that would happen after she video-called Ellis from your bathroom."

I shift forward in my seat, my elbows on my knees. "She did what?" I ask.

Griffin leans back in the chair, running a pale, tattooed hand through his dark hair. "Yeah, she was freaking out about kissing you or some shit. Said it was casual and an accident. I don't know, man, I wasn't supposed to talk to you about it, and Lennon is fucking scary." He shrugs. "Plus, it's not my business."

I chuckle, the black chair creaking as I sit back and fold my arms across my chest. "Yeah, okay. She's not as scary as I originally thought, but I get it."

"If you slept with her, what does that mean?" he asks.

My stomach twists at his words. *Accidental* might be true, but why does it have a bite to it? "Not much," I conceded. "Like she said, it was casual. A one-time thing. We're friends." The words taste like a lie.

Griffin's brow furrows. "Friends?"

"Yeah. I've been helping her around the house–fixing shit, I guess. She stayed over that night because there were bats in her chimney. We watched movies." I shrug. "The sex was a one-time thing. You don't need to worry about it."

He doesn't look convinced as Ryland strolls back over, throwing himself in one of the empty chairs. Griffin glances in his direction before pulling out his phone again and sending what looks to be a text message.

Shit.

"Shop opens in an hour," Ryan says. "Who's next?"

Nolan returns just in time to claim the spot, and I pull out my phone–trying to avoid Griffin's puzzled look.

He may not know about Alexis, but he sure as shit knows how my dates normally go. I don't linger–and I certainly don't invite women back to my fucking house. There's a contemplative expression on his face I don't want to acknowledge.

Helping around the house, allowing her to stay over, watching movies, having sex–it's all pretty damning.

Distracting myself by scrolling through my contacts, I land on Lennon's name–or maybe I sought it out, but I don't want to admit that.

> **Me:** So, listen.

Her response is almost immediate.

> **Lennon:** Ellis already called. It's fine. I told her we were just friends, but damn news travels fast with those two.

I chuckle, listening to Ryan explain placement for whatever tattoo he's doing next. I can still feel Griffin's gaze, but I choose to ignore it and type out my reply.

> **Me:** It's like they've become a package deal. Does Ellis know he got another tattoo this morning?

> **Lennon:** Awe, look at us. We're becoming our own little gossip package deal, too.

> **Lennon:** She does, by the way. You need to send me juicer gossip.

My chest feels tight as I stare at the screen. Something about that message sends a thrill through my blood. I like talking to Lennon, and the idea that we'd be some kind of a package deal. I enjoy spending hours with her discussing movies and books. Being around her feels simple–easy.

> **Me:** No real gossip over here.

> **Lennon:** I heard one of Griffin's friends has a green schlong.

I try and fail to suppress my laugh, thankful the buzz of the tattoo gun drowns the noise out a bit.

> **Me:** I heard the green schlong is massive and tastes great with vegetable dip.

> **Lennon:** Noah, I didn't know you were into such weird shit.

> **Me:** I'll try anything once.

I wince, realizing the double meaning. Somehow, the text feels all wrong. It makes it sound like I was just trying her out–seeing what the sex would be like without considering her. It makes me feel like an asshole. I type something out, staring at the message for a full minute before hitting send.

I'd do it again, by the way.

A confession plainly written. A risk, but I think we are beyond those.

My finger hovers over the send button for a moment before I press it.

Three dots flash on the screen. They disappear and reappear again. Finally, Lennon's text comes through, and I'm not sure how to take it.

Lennon: I'll see you tonight.

When I look up, I realize Griffin is staring at me from across the room. He tilts his head, raising his brows and clearly wanting an answer for what I'm doing. I shrug and pocket my phone.

And as much as I hate to admit it, I've never been more fucking excited about a bonfire in my life.

Seventeen

Lennon

"I have some friends coming over tonight. I'm just setting up."

I hold the phone between my shoulder and my ear as I pull the chocolate bars, marshmallows, graham crackers, and hot dogs from the grocery bag and place them onto the kitchen island. My sister and I aren't necessarily close, but we talk once in a while.

A ten-year age gap makes it difficult to grow up as if you aren't an only child. By the time I reached high school, Lorelei was long gone but not forgotten. My parents were so proud of my sister's drive and desire to become a doctor and made it clear at every turn.

They littered their conversations with praise of Lorelei's incredible work ethic, her honorable pursuits, the kindness and softness she exuded as a child. In contrast, my anger burned hot and fast as a child, my goals scattered and fully based on my emotions.

It wasn't until I fell in love with stories that I realized how much I wanted to know people. First books, then the front porch swing of an old neighbor across the street. She'd told me stories of her husband, a contractor who'd poured over the house with steady hands–adding the sunroom she loved so dearly to the back.

At every turn, I'd fallen in love with talking to people–learning about them.

I wanted to do something different.

My mom, though more supportive, has never had much of a backbone when it comes to my father. He's opinionated and brash–which is probably where I get those qualities. When I decided to major in business in the hopes that I'd create a space where stories were welcomed, it didn't seem to be good enough. Staying in Ohio and deciding against moving back to Minnesota? Not good enough. Buying this house? Also, not good enough.

My sister *did* help me get my job at the pediatric office, though. And while she isn't the warmest, I suppose I can't complain. I'm not really, either.

"Is the house even ready for guests?" she asks on the other line.

I huff a laugh–not as genuine as I'd like. "They're just friends. We are having a bonfire and hanging out. While I'm still working on renovations, the house has plenty of space for me to hang out with my friends."

I wad the grocery bags up and shove them into yet another grocery bag under the sink, closing the old cabinet before gripping my phone with my hand.

"Did you say you were doing most of the renovations yourself?" Lorelei asks.

"Yeah," I turn, leaning against the kitchen island and looking out the window to the yard. The barn looms over the dying grass, the red paint worn, and the doors somewhat sticky. I like the barn and the old wooden banister of the staircase. I like the *charm* of the house. Lorelei would certainly hate it, but I don't. My sister firmly subscribes to the sad millennial grey aesthetic.

"How's that going?" she asks. I suppose I could work harder at holding up my end of the conversation.

"It's good," I note. "I have–" I pause for a moment, trying to figure out what to call Noah exactly. *Fuck buddy* doesn't sound like anyone in my family would approve, but it also doesn't seem incredibly accurate. "I have a friend helping me out."

"Ellis knows about home renovations?"

"No." I laugh. "Ellis knows nothing about home renovations." I watch as a squirrel scurries across the yard, climbing up the trunk of the giant oak tree shading the side of the barn, the only tree before the treeline. "To be honest, Noah doesn't know much either, but he's been pretty helpful. Redid a lot of the porch yesterday, so I don't feel like I'll die whenever I–"

"He?" she interrupts, and I can almost see the curious expression on her face.

"He's a mutual friend." I lean against the counter, wincing.

"I thought you said he was *your* friend?" she prods.

I roll my eyes. "I didn't say those exact words."

"They were implied, Lennon. Are you finally dating? It would be great for you to bring someone around this Thanksgiving if you'll be in Minneapolis. I'm sure Devon would love to have someone other than dad to talk about sports with."

Somehow, I don't think Noah would enjoy talking about football the way Lorelei's boyfriend does. Even though Devon is an engineer with a salary more than I could ever dream of, he's a major sports guy. The kind to yell at the television every time a game is on–an activity he openly participates in at our house over the holidays.

"Noah might be more interested in talking about books than sports," I confess, without really having a right to. Noah's not visiting my family. He's just a friend I had sex with. That's all.

"Devon reads a lot of nonfiction. Is that what your guy reads?"

I blink. "He's not *my guy*. He is an English Professor at a local college. And the idea of him coming to Minneapolis to meet our family is wildly out of the realm of possibilities." I turn, stacking the chocolate bars on top of one another and then redoing the entire thing just to expel some energy. "Anyway, I need to go, Lor."

"That's fine." There's a pause on the line, and I expect her to hang up, but she doesn't. "Lennon?"

My brow furrows. "What?"

"Nevermind. Mom is on the other line. She probably wants me to pick her up that buckeye cake from the hospital again. I'm on call, and she never fails to request hospital food. Something I will never understand because it all tastes terrible to me."

I chuckle, glancing at the time on the microwave. It's nearly six, and Ellis and Cass should be here soon to help set up. "Better answer her. You know how she is."

I can hear the smile in her voice. "Needy as ever," she says before hanging up.

Standing in my new kitchen, I look at the shelf above the bottom cabinets littered with paper plates and plastic cups I've been using since the house didn't come with a dishwasher, and I got fucking tired of washing all my shit. I can see mismatched mugs and plates on that shelf–thrifted, most likely–and used to serve breakfast each morning.

The cabinets could use a fresh coat of paint, and I am pretty sure the lack of furniture throughout the house is going to be a problem. Moving from a small apartment to a large farmhouse really showed me how much space I *didn't* have.

I blink and look back out the window, noting the fire pit with lawn chairs set up around it. Noah should be here closer to seven, but I can't seem to stop thinking about how my sister just talked about him.

Would he watch football with my dad? Would my family even like someone like Noah? Aside from romantic spy novels, what *does* he read?

I pull out my phone, unable to help myself. His contact is a giant magnet, and unfortunately for me, I might just be made of metal.

> **Me:** Do you like football?

· · · ● · ● · ● · · ·

"You're telling me it's not going to be weird, but I feel like it still might be weird." Ellis leans over the kitchen island with a spoon and a jar of peanut butter–a delicacy she took to when we were in college.

I roll my eyes, gripping the edge of the counter across the sink to ground myself. Maybe Ellis is right. Maybe it *will* be weird with Noah here. After we slept together, we very nearly did it again. I'm also not sure how to interpret our texting conversations. He never responded to my question about football, so that says something.

Doesn't it?

"We're friends. It's fine."

"I don't know," Cass says from her spot across the kitchen and leaning against the stainless steel refrigerator. "I can fully admit that I don't know how my friends feel inside of me, and I think that's probably more normal."

I chuckle, trying to brush it off before the rest of the guests arrive. Somehow, this bonfire became bigger than I had originally thought. Griffin is in town with the band playing a few shows nearby. He leaves again in a few days. I decided to invite that whole crowd, plus his friend Ryan, Ryan's partner, and Noah, of course.

"Here's a question," Ellis starts. "What was the whole art show situation? You never fully told us what happened or why Noah was yelling on the porch."

You're the only one aside from my family that knows about my failed engagement.

"Noah used to know him through a former mutual friend. He was already married."

"Ew, gross." Ellis winces.

Cass sighs. "I'm not entirely convinced there are men out there who *don't* cheat." Her blue eyes flick to Ellis and widen. "Aside from Griffin, of course."

Ellis stands straight, looking uncomfortable as she places the spoon back into the jar of peanut butter. "Yeah, so about that–"

My head whips to her, and I'm pretty sure the speed at which it happens would put a poltergeist to shame. "I'll kill him," I say–fully meaning it.

"It's not that–" Ellis trails off, not finishing the sentence.

"Then what the fuck are you saying here."

She waves her hands around wildly. "I don't know!" she practically screeches. "Griffin's been acting a little weird! I'm not sure. There's no weird possessiveness over his phone or anything, but he's on the road a lot and the vibes are–I'm not sure."

There's a low hum of anger running through my veins at the thought that Griffin would do anything to compromise their relationship. I've never seen Ellis so happy–so willing to step out and try new things. She's always been anxious and somewhat of an overthinker. I like that Griffin's brought out this other side of her, but if he so much as breathes the wrong way in her presence–

"I'll get to the bottom of it," I assert, and Ellis rolls her eyes.

"Please don't," she says.

"I'll actually help!" Cass adds from where she's standing just as the doorbell rings.

We all head that direction, and I can't stop the small amount of nerves that decided to make an appearance, knowing that Noah might be the one at the door. I wipe my hands on my jeans and adjust the crewneck sweatshirt I threw on over my white t-shirt before walking down the hallway to the front door.

When I open it, Griffin stands with a pack of hard cider and a stupid fucking grin. I glare at him, hoping to ascertain whatever vibes might be *off*. "Griffin," I say, my tone like ice.

"Lennon," he responds before looking behind me. When he finds Ellis, it's hard to see anything but complete adoration, but I'm the one that went on a date with a fucking married man. How am I to know?

"I think we should have a chat," I say before Ellis steps in front of me, tucking herself beneath one of his arms and rolling her eyes.

"He should be right behind me," Griffin says before moving past me and disappearing down the hallway with Ellis.

A jolt runs through me when I find Noah walking across the gravel, wearing another one of his stupid fucking sweaters and a pair of slacks. I desperately want to take them off him–feel the hard planes of his chest with my fingers.

"Well," Cass whispers in my ear, gripping my arm. "I suddenly have to use the restroom."

She's gone before I can protest, and I'm left standing in the entryway with the man who I can't seem to stop thinking about.

"You never answered my question," I say by way of greeting.

Noah chuckles, that dimple popping out and making my knees weak. "Happy to see you too, Lennon."

I raise a brow. "Football?"

"I'm more of a soccer guy, really." He pushes his glasses up his nose, that smirk still lingering on his mouth–his bottom lip on display before me and ready to be kissed. I could pull it between my teeth–coax one of those delicious low groans from his throat.

My body feels flushed. "My dad hates soccer."

Noah looks puzzled, and my stomach drops. *What the fuck am I even saying?*

"Okay?" he questions. "Your dad is also an asshole, so I'm not sure what that has to do with anything."

I release a breathy laugh, one corner of my mouth turning upward.

"You guys coming?" Griffin shouts from the kitchen.

"Yeah," Noah yells back.

I tilt my head to the side. "Also," I start. "You know how we have our own little gossip thing going?" I lower my voice to a whisper. "Ellis said Griffin is acting weird." My eyes narrow, hoping like hell I'm intimidating enough to get the truth out of him. Somehow–I don't think Noah would lie to me. "Know anything about it?"

Noah steps closer, the scent of tobacco and vanilla making me dizzy. It must be his cologne, but it drags up memories I really shouldn't be thinking about. "Yeah, actually," he admits. "I do, but I'm not sure you won't Facetime Ellis from my fucking bathroom and ruin it."

I ignore the embarrassment that threatens to color my cheeks. "I'll tell Ellis if she needs to know. He's not fucking cheating, is he? Because I swear to fuck if–"

Noah's hand gently covers my mouth, the warmth of his skin seeping all the way to my bones as I stop talking. When he pulls his hand away, he leans closer, so close I can feel his breath on my face—spearmint and something that is so Noah. My stomach dips. "He's not cheating," he says. "Quite the opposite, actually."

My brow furrows. "The opposite of—"

Noah raises his brows.

"Oh." *Oh my god.* I think my entire soul is aglow. "He's proposing?" I whisper a little louder than I intended.

"Lennon, you have to shut up." Noah looks toward the hallway just as Ellis appears.

"You guys coming?" I can tell by her annoyed expression that we are taking too long and already making it weird. Maybe she was right.

My eyes want to water at the idea of Ellis getting married. She's always wanted a surprise engagement—something thoughtful and more private. In college, we'd talk about the what ifs and the maybe somedays. There's no way I can tell her—it'll ruin everything, and for some reason, in this moment, Noah trusts me.

"Yeah," I say, forcing myself to appear normal and unfazed. "Yeah, we can grab the hot dogs and take them outside. I'm pretty sure there are enough skewers."

I can't look at her when I push past her, needing to gather myself and stop being such a hopeless romantic—a sensitive fucking baby.

"What did you tell her?" I hear Ellis ask Noah from behind me.

"That I don't like football," he says by way of answer before following us all to the kitchen.

Eighteen

Noah

I shouldn't have told Lennon.

I recognize it was an idiotic decision, but the idea that Ellis would think anything negative about whatever Griffin is doing didn't sit right with me.

And I trust Lennon.

For whatever reason.

The stars peek out overhead as Ryland strums a guitar across the crackling bonfire. Everyone is laughing, lost in conversation, when

Lennon plants herself on the log beside me, a skewer and marshmallow in hand.

"I'm not going to tell," she affirms before piercing the marshmallow and holding it out over the fire. "I wouldn't ruin something like that for my best friend."

I watch as the glow of the fire dances over her features, touching everything I had the privilege of touching just yesterday. I'm jealous of the light, watching as the cool autumn breeze picks up a strand of her hair. Without much thought, I reach out and tuck it behind her ear.

Surprisingly, Lennon doesn't pull away. She just turns to look at me, those green eyes vibrant under the vast night sky.

I clear my throat. "I didn't think you would."

There's a pause before she speaks again. "I need to start picking out more furniture for the house. I'm thinking of thrifting most of it, but there are a few things I may just want to pick up for ease. Are you any good at putting bookshelves together?"

I chuckle, running a hand through my hair and looking back at the fire where her marshmallow is hovering. "That is one thing I have experience with," I admit.

I can hear the satisfied smile in her voice. "Good."

Ryland's playing ceases as he nears the end of a song. When he starts strumming again, the song wraps around the fire and mingles with the quiet conversations.

"I'm supposed to go back to my family's around Thanksgiving," Lennon says, slowly turning the marshmallow to toast the other side. "Apparently, my sister has decided she's excited to see me."

I lean forward, wringing my hands together. "Are we supposed to be happy about that?" I ask.

Lennon winces. "I don't know. I guess it's good. She hasn't taken much of an interest in my life–busy, I suppose. Recently, her newest hobby consists of hounding me with questions. She asked about the inn and my love life, but none of it feels–" She shrugs. "It's not warm, you know?"

"I can buy you a heated blanket." I smile, turning my head to look at her. "Should take care of that."

Lennon laughs, and I long to drown in the sound of it. "Yeah, okay." She shifts on the log, moving closer. "I might be letting my dad's comments get in the way of a relationship with her. It's just weird feeling like you're living in someone else's shadow and not measuring up. Especially because she's just so–"

"Cold?" I offer.

"Shut up."

"Never." My chest pulls tight. Something about Lennon talking to me about this feels important–like she doesn't frequently open up. Getting to know her is a gift. "You could be right, but I am not one to talk being an only child."

"You must be real selfish, Noah." She nudges me with her shoulder.

I can't stop the smile from dancing on my lips. "Yeah, pretty much. Minus the fact that when my parents get old and die, I'll have to do it alone."

Her face twists. "Oof, okay."

I laugh quietly, watching as Ellis leans into Griffin across the way, the two of them in their own world. Cass, Ryan, and his partner are listening to Ryland play. It's a weird feeling that strikes me as I realize the circle of friends I've created–the one without Alexis.

Lennon pulls the perfectly browned marshmallow from near the fire and examines it before grabbing a graham cracker and piece of chocolate from the chair next to her. She quickly assembles the dessert while Griffin says something across the fire that makes everyone else laugh.

"Those are better burnt," I say.

"You're a fucking idiot," she says without hesitation, and this time, it's my turn to nudge her shoulder.

"Sure, I am," I say. "I've been meaning to ask. Why did you video call Ellis from my bathroom?"

She turns to me; the s'more gripped between her finger and her thumb. "Girl stuff."

"You told her we kissed."

"So?" she asks. "They already know we fucked, Noah. I think we are past that."

My eyes flick to her lips on instinct, and I note the way she sucks in a breath. We're sitting close–too close–trapped in our own little world around the fire. "I meant what I said," I whisper. "I'd do it again."

Before she can respond, Cass stands up from her spot, holding a large tote bag. "So," she begins, her blue eyes lighted. "I found some flashlights at the dollar store the other day. Not sure if they'll work, but I was thinking we have enough people to play flashlight tag. Why the fuck not? It's dark out here anyway."

"I'm down," Ryan says, reaching for the bag and grabbing a flashlight out of it. He tests that it works and grins.

"What do we do?" Griffin starts. "Hide around the property or whatever."

"Yes, exactly," Cass answers.

"Okay," Lennon starts, whipping her hands on the grass. "You guys can use the house or the barn. There's a short trail over by the woods that I plan on clearing more of. Just be careful because I don't know what is out there, but it should be fun."

Ryland flicks the latch on his guitar case, his sandy blonde hair falling across his brow. "Sounds like fun," he says before getting up to grab a flashlight from the bag, too.

We all take turns testing to make sure they work before establishing that Griffin will be it to start.

Once we are all standing and ready, Griffin yells to go from the other side of the house, and I take off toward the barn, flashlight off and nothing but the starlight to guide me—which fucking sucks because I stumble over at least four random holes in the yard. I make a note to fix those for Lennon before grabbing the old wooden door and attempting to pry it open.

The door sticks when I pull on it. Muscles straining, I throw my body weight into it and curse when the rusty tracks of the sliding barn door screech.

I consider finding a new spot, but with the clock still ticking, I enter the musty barn. In the darkness, it's hard to make out anything aside from the dirt floors littered with hay and the scent of aged timber. The wooden ladder to my left seems promising, and I grip the creaking wood, testing the bottom rung before ascending toward the hayloft. The loft seems safe enough for walking, and the twenty bales of straw stacked sporadically provide a nice cover. Finding a small alcove in between the bales, I stand with my back against the wooden wall of the barn.

Cobwebs ghost over my forearm, and I wipe them away, shaking off what feels like fifty years of dust.

When a light shines through the cracks in the wall toward the barn, my stomach sinks. Of course, this would be the first fucking place he'd look. I'm a thirty-two-year-old man, and I can't fucking figure out this childish game.

"Ouch." A soft voice sounds from below, and I still. Footsteps up the ladder, a light streaking across the ground floor of the barn, and my heart kicks up a notch.

She's headed straight for the hayloft.

"Shit." I smile, recognizing Lennon's whispered curse just before she shoves herself into the small alcove I've found, her eyes widening when she spots me.

I'm not fucking losing this game.

Tugging at her arm gently, I spin her around, pulling her in until her back presses to mine. She pushes further, her ass against my cock, and her hair tickling my nose. The scent of amber and vanilla fills my nostrils. There's a touch of sweetness to it, drowning out the smell of old hay and dust.

She must have worn perfume.

"He's going to find us," she whispers, gripping the darkened flashlight in one hand.

My grip on her tightens, holding her even closer as my nose brushes against her ear. I whisper, trying to keep my voice as quiet as possible, noting that Griffin has entered the barn and is currently searching the bottom level, wading through random storage items. "He will if you don't stop talking," I say. "You need to be quiet, Lennon."

"Don't tell me what to do," she snaps, her voice a hushed whisper. The softness of the skin at her neck, the scent of her perfume, the curve of her ass–it all sends a pleasant buzz over my skin. I'm hyper aware of every place our bodies touch–the ways they've touched in the past. My hands slide to her hips, holding her to me. When she shifts, grinding gently against my cock, I fight off a groan. There's no way I'm going to be able to hide what this is doing to me.

Fuck.

"You didn't seem to mind that the other day," I add, and she freezes.

For a moment, I'm afraid I've said the wrong thing. Maybe yesterday was too much. Maybe she's regretting the whole thing.

My fingers loosen where I grip her.

"Those were entirely different circumstances," she whispers. "Now shut up, or he's going to find us."

I fight the chuckle that threatens to break free, enjoying the feel of her when she pushes closer.

Nineteen

Lennon

Griffin finishes checking the ground floor of the barn, but never bothers climbing the ladder. My heart pounds in my chest as Noah's hand grips my waist from where we are hidden, surrounded by straw. The scratch of the straw pokes through the arm of my sweater, bales stacked on either side of us, shrouding us in darkness.

When Griffin leaves, I don't move. Noah's breath warms my neck, matching the rhythm of his chest behind me. We still, as if we are waiting for something to happen.

What we're waiting for, I have no idea.

I suck in a deep breath, noting the way his fingers tighten infinitesimally on my hips. Another breath–another, and all of my senses heighten. The smell of him, the feel of his skin–his nearness–

"We're in the clear," he whispers, leaning closer, and I shiver.

I don't want to move from this spot. I don't want to stop feeling his hands on me. Somehow, having sex with him has just made my desire increase. All I want is *more*–more of his humor, his presence–all of it.

"I know," I say, leaning back into him. He takes the hint, his lips ghosting over my neck. The soft press of his mouth drags a soft sound from my parted lips.

I place my hand over his at my hip and press until his fingers pull me closer, my ass firmly against him. He's been hard this whole time, and something about that has my body crying out with need.

"What is it you want?" he asks, the timbre of his voice sending goosebumps over my skin. Noah kisses my shoulder over my sweatshirt, one hand moving to my stomach with his fingers splayed out and taunting beneath the fabric.

I grind back into him, unable to control my breath.

"Anyone could come up here," he warns.

I lean back, resting my head against his chest. "I've changed my mind," I whisper. "You can tell me to be quiet, now."

He chuckles as his hand drags over my skin, fingers toying with the waistline of my jeans. When he pushes lower, I groan.

"That's not what you're supposed to be doing." He doesn't relent, placing another kiss near my throat. "Should I talk you through this?"

My breath catches, and I grind back into him, forcing a sound to sneak past his lips. I'm high on it. I want to hear it again.

"Go ahead," I say. "I need to know what you're doing."

Noah's other hand trails up my arm and makes me curse the cooler weather for the first time all autumn. I want his fingers on my skin, and it isn't until his hand is at my throat, slowly brushing over the spot he kissed with his thumb, that I get what I want. "I'm going to touch you, Lennon. Is that alright?"

"Please," I practically beg as the hand by my stomach finds the button of my jeans, unhooking it and slowly dragging the zipper downward.

"You said you like the build-up," he whispers, the hand at my throat moving to my hip and pulling me tight against him. His other hand glides lower, his fingers tucking beneath my underwear, but he's nowhere near where I need him. In fact, he feels miles away.

"Where should I go from here?" he whispers again, and there's a taunting to his voice that's driving me crazy. "Should I push my fingers into you?" I'm panting. "Use the heel of my hand to drive you wild?"

"Just fucking touch me, Noah." My hand reaches up, wrapping around the back of his neck as I attempt to pull him even closer—as if that's even possible.

"Are you begging?" he chides. "I didn't take you as the type to beg." His hand moves lower, so close now that I can hardly breathe.

"I'm begging." My hips grind against him, relishing in the sound he makes. "I'm not above begging for your fingers inside of me."

Noah practically growls as his fingers finally make their way to where I need him most, entering and curling as his palm rubs against me, and my breath catches. Pulse pounding, I lean into every drag of his palm against me, my hips moving–guiding.

"*Christ,*" I whisper.

"Are you praying?" he asks.

"Fuck, no."

I moan with each motion of his hand, pleasure directing my focus to where he touches me. My body climbs higher with every second until I can feel myself on the edge–wet and desperate. Noah's teeth scratch over the skin below my ear, making me shudder. My legs shake, and I'm so close, I can hardly speak.

"I can't get enough of you," he whispers, and I squeeze my eyes shut, the tension finally releasing.

I'm left panting and wanting more than anything to drive him wild. Noah removes his hand from my pants and I zip them. When they're buttoned, I turn around with the sharp need to make him come undone in this musty barn.

Noah watches me slowly lower to my knees, looking up through my lashes when my hand glides up his thigh. "No jeans today?" I question, tilting my head to the side. I pull my bottom lip between my teeth, fighting off the smile that threatens to pull at my mouth. He looks thoroughly wound up–needy.

His only response is a whispered *fuck* just before the barn door slides open more abruptly, multiple flashlights illuminating the darkness.

"Shit," I mutter, quickly standing and stepping away.

"Where the fuck are they?" Ryan asks, and I listen as footsteps creak on the rungs of the wooden ladder to the hayloft.

I back out of the alcove, a bright light flashing in my face as Ellis stands there, her eyes wide.

Lifting my hand, I squint against the light before she lowers it, gaping.

When I take a step back, my ass brushes against something hard, and I realize Noah is standing directly behind me. I can't imagine how we look. Guilty isn't enough to cover it.

The heat of embarrassment washes over my chest–my face, and I fight the urge to run. There's no getting out of this one. "Hey," I say, trying like hell to keep my tone casual.

"Found them," Ellis calls over her shoulder, and Griffin laughs below.

"*Them?*" he questions, and I can hear the mirth in his tone.

Noah clears his throat, and I move forward, keeping my expression pleasant and absolutely not guilty. I'm trying to give off *I totally wasn't having sex* vibes, but somehow, I think I'm failing.

I pass Ellis, turning to scale down the ladder in an attempt to get away as quickly as possible. "Who lost?" I ask.

"Nolan," Ryland says from below. "But I think we might be done playing games at this point."

I step onto the dirt floor of the bar, turning with a questioning look on my face. "Why?" I ask, tilting my head as Ellis and then Noah join us on the ground floor.

Griffin turns, hiding the laughter that's clearly threatening to break free. When his eyes flick back and forth between me and Noah, I try not to wince. "You really don't want us to answer that," he says.

Twenty

Noah

My coffee's gone cold.

Which is a damn shame because after a long day of classes and a faculty meeting, I'm not ready to teach my Friday night class. It's only an hour and a half, but I can imagine that college students don't like having class from six to seven-thirty on a Friday night either. It's one semester, though.

I glance at the stack of graded papers that were dropped on my desk earlier today and decide against looking at them. After the busy day I've had, they can wait until next week.

Opening my phone, I find the group text titled *No Nuts No Glory*, and shoot a text to what is now Ryan, Griffin, Ryan's partner, Wyatt, and the entire band Griffin works for.

> **Me:** Anyone up for the bar tomorrow? The one with arcade games so I can kick all your asses at Pac-Man.

Before I close out of my messages, a text from Lennon pops up, making my entire body buzz again with the memory of last weekend. We've texted daily, neither one of us mentioning what happened in the barn. There's been a heavy dose of flirting, but I can't bring myself to be the first to break. She'd been clear that the sex would be just that–*sex*. I'm not sure what we did counts as breaking our *only one time* rule, but I don't want to find out.

With our physical relationship off the table, we've texted about numerous unrelated topics. Music, childhood memories, books, our jobs–anything and everything.

> **Lennon:** Been busy today? If you're up for it this weekend, I need to shop around for some furniture. I need an expert.

I chuckle, typing out a response.

> **Me:** I just invited the guys to hang out to-morrow, but Sunday is open. I can pencil you in.

> **Me:** As for busy, I haven't even had dinner yet, and I have a class in ten.

> **Lennon:** I can bring you something?

Lennon: I want to see you.

Me: Sure. Done at seven-thirty.

Pocketing my phone, I grab my bag and lock up the office, heading toward the room at the end of the hall where the majority of my class is already seated and chatting.

Distracted and somewhat flustered, I set my laptop up on the podium.

My carefully crafted love-life only remained possible through clear communication and hard boundaries. With Lennon, every rule has gotten up, and jumped out the window, never to be seen again.

The worst part is I *like* talking to her. The more I learn about the original hardwood floors, the heights etched into the door to the basement, and the banister that Lennon seems so infatuated with, the more I uncover about *her*.

Lennon loves to create stories about the people who used to live in the farmhouse. I added that she's one Ouija board away from talking to them herself, and she informed me that if I brought such a thing near her, she'd never speak to me again.

And I desperately need her to keep talking to me.

I look up at my students seated around the old classroom. Hardwood floors, crown moulding, and creaking–everything. The classroom and my office exist in the oldest building on campus. She'd love it.

"Christ, don't you guys have better things to do than sit in class on a Friday evening?" I ask, and soft laughter flits around the room.

"Yeah, actually," Cole says from the corner. Cole's on the baseball team and frequently flirts with the girls in my class, but he's a decent kid, secretly enjoys the subject matter, too. "How about you cancel class?" he asks, a crooked smile on his face.

I sigh. "Can't." Clicking around on my laptop, I find the presentation that goes with today's lesson. "Unfortunately for all of you, I would like to discuss the cultural significance of *Lord of the Flies*."

Maggie, one of the students toward the front, makes a small sound, all the color draining from her face. "I thought we were reading *Emma*?"

I grin as the presentation for the exact book she's talking about pops up on the screen. "Gotcha."

Groans erupt across the room.

The projector slowly focuses as the first slide of my presentation appears. "So," I start before taking a sip of the cold coffee clutched in my hand. "I'd like to continue talking about themes present in the novel. Last week, we discussed bias as a theme. Emma had an idea of what she believed about Mr. Elton and Harriet, and so everything she saw had been viewed through that lens. What other themes do you find evident in the text?"

Paige sits up, her straight, brown hair smooth–not a single strand out of place. I recall reading her essay about the last assigned book we discussed in this class. Her attention to detail happens to be equal parts impressive and disconcerting. "The lack of transparent communication," she interjects.

I clear my throat, nodding once. "Good. Okay." My fingers fumble with the stray pen left on the podium, impulsively clicking the end a few times. My phone feels heavy in my pocket–taunting.

I look at Paige. "Go on."

She beams. "Well, for one, the novel is full of miscommunication. Not only did we find bias in Emma, but overall, the social propriety led to a lot of heartache for the characters. Honestly, if they had one singular honest conversation, maybe Emma would have spent less time matchmaking and more time realizing she'd been in love with Mr. Knightly all along."

My collar feels too tight, but I don't let my discomfort show. I make it a point to keep my personal life out of my lessons, but this one has taken an unfortunate turn. Bringing my coffee to my lips, I urge them to continue.

Cole chuckles, leaning back casually in his seat. "Sure, but then there wouldn't be a story. Besides, I'm not even sure Emma *realized* what she truly wanted."

Maggie grins, glancing back toward him. "Or she just convinced herself her life had been comfortable for fear of leaving her father in the event she married."

Rolling his tongue along his cheek, Cole sits forward, elbows resting on the wooden table. "Maybe if Mr. Knightley and Emma boned way sooner, she wouldn't have spent so much time lying to herself."

I choke on my coffee, setting it down before interjecting. "Interesting take. Not necessarily true." I push the sleeves of my sweater up, suddenly way too hot. "Emma did not want to marry for many reasons. Her father, the estate. I don't believe those were excuses but practical reasons to avoid such a thing. Complications provide a decent deterrent."

Cole's shit-eating grin tells me I'm not going to like what he says next. "You're married, right Professor Ashwood?"

I frown. "I am not. Nor do I make it a habit of discussing my personal life with my students."

Paige giggles, and I tap the pencil against the podium.

"Miscommunication serves a purpose in literature, but beyond that," I begin, taking the reins. "It's a more accurate reflection of real life."

• • • ● • ● • ● • •

When class ends, I know it's late based on the darkened hallways and the lingering exhaustion weighing heavily on me.

The beginning of class sent my mind racing with questions I didn't want to answer.

Maybe if Mr. Knightley and Emma boned way sooner.

I scoff. As it seems, having sex can actually add more complexity than clarity, though I have wondered.

I gave up a lot following my failed relationship, made excuses, one might say. The thought of easing into something with Lennon, a date, perhaps, doesn't cause my skin to itch with discomfort.

An entirely new feeling.

Maybe Cole had been onto something.

I unlock my office, expecting Lennon within the next hour, so I try to respond to a few emails, tackle the grading I refused to look at earlier, and take a second to decompress.

When my phone vibrates on the dark wooden desk, I instantly snatch it, hoping it's her.

The number that flashes on the screen causes my brows to furrow.

I don't have it saved–but I remember it just the same.

Alexis.

I debate whether or not I should answer it for a solid three minutes before deciding to pick up despite the twisting in my gut. Her presence sucks the energy right out of the room.

"Hello?"

"I got your message." No hello, no pleasantries, just her irritation, and my uncomfortable emotions. I sent that message as a courtesy, but I'm now rethinking the decision. It looks bad. It *is* bad. I'm not sure why I cared to begin with.

"That would be the point," I say, tapping a pen on the shining wood of my desk. The coolness of her voice sets me on edge, anger simmering beneath the surface.

"How fucking dare you."

She's mad–incredibly so, and I flinch. Definitely not the right decision.

"Alexis–" I start, but she cuts me off.

"Is this some sad attempt at ruining my marriage out of jealousy or something?" She's fuming, and I can't say I blame her. I thought I'd done well phrasing it, but apparently not. A huge fucking mistake, that's what sending that message was. "Noah, I know I fucked up, but it's been five years. It's time to get over it and move on. I don't know why you had to come out of the blue. Hayes is pissed."

Rightfully so.

"Excuse me?" I say, ready to add more, but she doesn't cease.

"We weren't a match. You were focused on school and your career and hardly made time for me. Can you really blame me for what I did?"

What the fuck?

"I felt pressured to say yes to you because my family was there. But let's face it, we didn't have anything in common. Now I'm *happy,* and you decide to come in and fuck it all up."

"That's not–"

"It is!" she snaps. "That is exactly what is happening. I can't *believe* you decided to send me anything. I can't believe you thought you had the right to do something like that."

I lean back in the chair, staring at the bookshelf in my office and wishing I could sink down into the earth to disappear for a while. She's right. It has been five years, but something like that will scar you.

And while the skin around that scar feels numb and strange, her words still cut just the same. I wasn't cut out for marriage. There are a million things she said to me that come to the surface and remind me of my inadequacy.

I haven't directly thought about wanting *more* with Lennon until tonight. I've refused to touch that idea despite it dancing within reach, and as I listen to Alexis, I realize exactly why.

Lennon and I are better off as friends.

"I just thought you should know about Hayes, Alexis." My tone has gone cold–detached.

"And how did *you* know anything? Because he's informed me that it's all made up, and I'm inclined to believe him over my failure of an ex."

Ouch.

"He showed up at an art show with a friend of mine," I say, running a hand down my face.

"A friend?" She huffs. "A friend you've slept with? Don't think I haven't heard about how you spend your time, Noah. It's some girl you're fucking?"

I'm not understanding where she's going with this, nor do I care to continue listening to her. Those words sting, though. *It's some girl you're fucking* doesn't feel right. Reducing Lennon to that feels inherently wrong. It doesn't match what I'm feeling–what we're doing.

Or does it?

"I shouldn't have told you," I confess, as a sad attempt to placate her.

"Fucking hell, Noah," she spews. "Grow up!"

The phone cuts out, and I'm left with my thoughts. What she said *was* wrong. Lennon and I are friends. Then again, we haven't talked through what we are doing or why we are doing it. I finger fucked her in a barn after asserting that we were just friends and wouldn't make things weird for anyone.

There's a small part of me that feels like I'm doing her a disservice. Sure, Hayes was an asshole, but Lennon was on a date–she was pursuing a relationship, and that's something I haven't offered her. We've spent so much time together over the last month. I'm certain I'm holding her back. What if that's what she wants, and I'm just distracting her? An obstacle to her happiness?

"Knock, knock."

I look up to find Lennon walking into my office, a bag of takeout in her hand. "Hey," I say, trying like hell to hide how fucked I'm feeling.

"Wow, you *do* look tired." She sits down in the chair across from me, setting the bag on my desk and opening it to place food containers in front of me. "I didn't know exactly what you'd want, so there's a lot here. Hopefully, you'll find something."

"Where did you go?" I ask.

"Just the pub in that little town that is down the road from here. They had a bit of everything. I don't know." Her brows furrow as she grabs plastic silverware from the bag, looking unsure of herself. It's adorable.

"I trust your taste completely," I say, popping the lid off one of the containers.

We eat dinner in my office, talking about the past week. Lennon's back to working at the pediatric office, and I can tell she hates it. Especially when the conversation shifts to her plans for opening the bed-and-breakfast next summer. She talks about the mounds of paperwork, the scratch across the hardwood in one of the guest bedrooms upstairs, and I make a note to take a look at it the next time I'm over.

"You leave for Thanksgiving next month, right?" It's more than six weeks away, but I know she was nervous about it–could tell as much when she brought it up at the bonfire.

"Yeah," she says, placing the lid back on her container of food. "I'm trying to get as much done as I can before I go. I need to show something for myself."

"What if I go with you?" The words are out before I can stop them, and I realize my heart is racing in my chest. What the fuck am I even saying?

I just spent thirty minutes in my office brooding because I didn't think I could be whatever Lennon wanted. Maybe that's true, but maybe I could try. I've seen the bed-and-breakfast. I know how hard she's worked. I could be a buffer.

The look on her face has me second-guessing.

"What," she says.

"I could go as a friend. I don't know, I've seen what you've done with the house. I could compliment all of your grand achievements every chance I get–put your father in his place."

She smiles. "That's kind of hot." Lennon taps a finger on my desk. "And you mean your efforts," she says. "You're the one fixing everything."

"It's a teamwork thing," I say, winking.

Lennon shifts in her chair, and I wish I knew what she was thinking. "What about your family, or whatever?" she says. "If you're being serious."

I wave a hand. "My parents do a couple's getaway every year for Thanksgiving. I think it's because I haven't given them grandkids yet. Don't worry; I see them often enough. My mom always plans dinner the week before. You're welcome to come."

Her green eyes fix to mine, a question there that neither of us asks.

"Do you even want kids?" she asks, and my stomach sinks.

For some reason, I can't offer anything but honesty to her. "I did," I say. "I *was* engaged, remember? I wanted a lot of things I wasn't exactly cut out for."

Lennon's head tilts to the side, those eyes blazing in a way that makes me feel seen. It's almost too much.

"Who told you that?" she asks, and silence echoes in the room.

Another knock sounds from the door as Julia pokes her head in, and my eyes widen.

Lennon turns, staring at her.

"Hey," Julia says, her eyes flicking between Lennon and me. I'm not sure how to navigate this situation because if she's here, if she's in town again, there's only one thing she really wants.

"This is Lennon," I offer, floundering. "We have mutual friends."
Fuck.

If she's hurt, Lennon doesn't show it, and something about that bothers me. We were just talking about spending time with each other's families, and now we are here–lost in some weird relation-ship purgatory.

"Hey," she says. "My best friend is marrying his." Lennon tilts her head in my direction, the words creating more distance between us–like she doesn't want Julia to know our history–that I've been inside her.

Maybe she's embarrassed.

"Nice to meet you," Julia offers before her eyes meet mine. "I was wondering if you wanted some company tonight, but if you're working on best man duties, or whatever."

"I–"

Lennon stands up, gathering her half of the food and bagging it quickly. "I should go," she says, and I can't get a good read on how she's feeling. Usually it's written plainly across her face, but she's gone cold. "I haven't told Ellis he's proposing, by the way. But we can chat more about–" she pauses, her face twisting just briefly. It's at that exact moment I know I've fucked up. "We can talk about wedding details or something."

Lennon's gone before my brain can even catch up, leaving Julia standing in the doorway with a puzzled look on her face.

"That was incorrect, wasn't it," she says. "I'm sorry, I didn't real-ize–" She's fumbling for words. "I guess it's been a few weeks since I was here last. I flew out for another talk, and I am just a bit confused right now."

I clear my throat, closing my laptop and collecting my things. "I'm sorry," I say, because I am. "I'm not free tonight." My eyes meet hers when I stand up and put my bag over my shoulder. "I'm actually not free any night, really." I wince.

Julia chuckles before chewing on her cheek. "Yeah," she says. "Yeah, that's fine. I'll see you around or something."

She leaves the room too, and it feels like the oxygen has finally returned to the room, restoring my frontal lobe.

I should text Lennon; I know this. But I also know that she has never expressed a desire to be anything more. Maybe if I text her, it'll freak her out.

I've spent the entire day engrossed in my work, vacillating between the possibility of wanting a relationship with her and realizing I'd be shit at it.

I run my hand down my face, the tension tightening in my shoulders. Maybe I *should* try to just communicate. There's only one thing I know for sure, and it's that I don't know what the fuck I'm doing.

Twenty-One

Lennon

When I was in the tenth grade, my dad took me golfing with him. To be fair, I had no interest in golfing. I think I was just looking for an excuse to spend time with him.

The best part of that trip was riding in the golf cart.

I remember telling my dad about my bed-and-breakfast idea. It was something I'd started researching on my own because I'd become obsessed with the idea of owning a cozy house and becoming an innkeeper.

That was the first time my dad's attitude toward my future shifted.

Growing up, he was very much the *be anything you want* dad until I became a sophomore in high school. Lorelei was in med school, and I vividly remember my father telling me I should pursue something else. There was no sugarcoating it. He flat-out told me it would be frivolous and silly.

As the years passed, he insisted that I at least go to college to earn a degree–probably hopeful I'd change my mind about the whole thing.

It's like he genuinely believed I woke up one day and decided to throw my life into the toilet.

I wonder what he'd think if he saw me now.

Looking down at the messages in my phone, I realize that I may have made a brash decision when I downloaded the dating app last night after leaving Noah's office.

High on unwarranted hurt, I found myself swiping right on so many men I'd forgotten the original requirements by the end of it. 'Hasn't killed anyone' seemed like a good standard, but even then, some of my matches were questionable.

I ended up having a conversation with a guy named Reece. He had tattoos and a guitar, and since things seem to be working out so well with Ellis and Griffin, I figured music could be my new passion.

Or I was just looking for someone to take the burning away in my chest.

Noah and I aren't anything–so I'm not sure why seeing that woman walk into his office hurt so much–why what he said hurt so much.

He didn't technically lie to her.

Still, after a week of discussing nearly everything about myself, I couldn't help but question his reaction in that office. He hadn't even introduced me as a friend–which we had clearly stated we were. *Mutual friends.* The words taunt me as I run my hands through the gentle waves in my hair.

My dad constantly reminded me that the things I was doing weren't as honorable or noble–near worthless. What would he say knowing I not only failed in choosing a successful career path, but in beginning a relationship as well.

Worst of all, I hate myself for even considering what his opinion would be.

A knock sounds at the door, and I quickly glance at myself in the mirror. The burgundy corduroy skirt hits higher on my thighs than I'd like, so I opted for black sheer tights beneath it, a black long sleeve shirt, a cropped leather jacket, and a pair of short booties.

I sincerely hope I don't look like I'm trying too hard.

I don't even care about the guy.

When I get to the door, Reece is standing there, and I'm thankful that he looks more or less like the photos on the dating app.

"Hi, it's nice to meet you," I say, noting the way his eyes travel down my legs and then back up again.

"You still good with that one bar? There are arcade games. I thought it could be fun."

I smile, quickly swiping to share my location with Cass and Ellis before pocketing my phone. They know I'm on a date, and I got a million questions–most involving Noah's name–but I decided to ignore that. The important part is that if Reece kills me, they'll know what happened.

"Yeah," I say, pulling my bag over my shoulder. "That sounds great."

• • • ● • ● • ● • • •

Reece is nice enough, I suppose.

He didn't open my door for me, but he made good conversation in the car. When I talked about my favorite band, he handed me the AUX cord and listened to three songs in a row. It's a green flag, if I've ever seen one, but somehow I couldn't care less.

When we walk into the bar, the blaring music mixes with voices and the sound of the giant Jenga set falling. The scent of beer and fries make my mouth water, the tension leaving my shoulders until I spot him. Noah sits at a table with Ryan, Nolan, Wyatt, and one of the band members whose name I can't remember.

I swallow, ignoring his presence and continuing my date as Reece offers to grab me a beer.

Standing by the Pac-Man machine, Reece hands me a bottle. "You played this before?" he asks, and my eyes drift briefly to the table where Noah sits, abruptly flicking away as I chastise myself.

"Pac-Man?" I question. "Who hasn't."

He chuckles, and I decide that he isn't so bad—even if his car was the most beat-up vehicle I've ever seen in my life.

After one beer and a few rounds, I finally settle in. I don't look at Noah except for every few minutes to check that he's still there. Each time, he doesn't even look at me, so I assume that's a good sign.

It's clear communication, really. Becoming too attached to Noah will end with me getting hurt. He has no feelings for me aside from physical attraction. If he did, he wouldn't have made those comments in his office.

Ignoring the sting of that, I look at Reece setting his beer down on the empty stool near the game machine. "Want to switch it up?" he asks, his blonde hair falling across his brow, gray eyes muted in the bar lights.

"Sure, I was just thinking–"

"Lennon." Noah stands beside me, and I stop talking. I didn't even notice he had moved across the room. Straightening my spine, I steel myself.

Reece looks visibly confused, and I know it's petty as the words leave my mouth, but it's exactly why I say them.

"Hey!" I face Reece, gesturing to Noah without really looking at him. "This is Noah. We have mutual friends."

I swear he flinches next to me, and I curse myself for tracking anything he's doing at all.

"Oh, cool," Reece says, holding out a hand. "I'm Reece."

Noah doesn't return the gesture. He glances at Reece's hand and leaves it at that. Reece, clearly uncomfortable, grabs his empty beer bottle and holds it up. "I'm going to get another one of these," he says before placing a kiss to the side of my head. It's somewhat awkward–more than he's done all night, but I accept it, somewhat pleased when I see Noah's dark eyes narrow.

He's wearing jeans again, a gray shirt and a flannel unbuttoned over it, and I roll my eyes. Of course, he added a leather watch to the ensemble. It's *Noah*.

"You're pissed," he observes, and I turn away to start a new game on the console.

"Am I?"

He scoffs, stepping closer as I peek back at Reece, where he stands by the bar. "Why are you pissed, Lennon?"

My brows furrow, and I grip the joystick harder, quickly navigating the stupid fucking maze where this yellow fucking creature has to outrun the stupid fucking ghosts. "I'm not pissed," I say, changing direction to go after the larger yellow orbs so I can eat those fuckers instead. "I'm on a date. Which you are ruining, by the way." I laugh, but the sound is tight and clearly not the casual approach I wanted to take. "Maybe that's what I'm pissed about."

Noah leans in, the smell of his cologne invading my nostrils as images of him sitting by the fire and sprawled out on my bed flash unbidden in my mind.

His voice drops lower, the room narrowing until every inch of space feels taken up by just the two of us. "Do you hear yourself?" he questions.

I match his question with one of my own. "Why are you over here?"

"Why are you on a date?"

Pac-Man dies, and I don't even bother to plan his sad funeral. I push the joystick upward, a bit too forcefully, and turn to face Noah head-on. "Because I want to be!" I say, my voice rising. "What the fuck, Noah?" I try to calm my racing heart, but his nearness, his *nosiness*–

I lift my chin. "Why are you bothering me? Didn't you have a hook-up last night?"

There it is.

Showing all my fucking cards all at once.

I should be embarrassed.

"No," he says, his voice cold. "No, I didn't."

I roll my eyes, wanting to believe him so badly. It's physically painful. "Right." The word drips with sarcasm.

Noah places his hands on the console on either side of me, so close I'm helpless to do anything but look up and notice his intense gaze.

Caged in with the scent of tobacco leaf and vanilla swirling around me, inhibiting my judgment, I suck in a breath.

"I asked her to leave," he says. "We didn't–" He looks away briefly. "I haven't slept with anyone else or been around anyone but you in weeks." He glances back to the bar, finding Reece easily before standing straight with his arms at his side. The tense line of his jaw makes me want to reach out and touch him. "Why are you on a date with him?" he asks.

I watch Noah track the guy, realizing what's actually going on. "Are you jealous?" I ask, one corner of my mouth turning upward.

Deep satisfaction washes over me–shameful but pleasant as Noah stares daggers at my date.

Noah's gaze flicks to mine. "Yeah, I'm fucking jealous," he practically growls.

His honesty surprises me, and my eyes widen. We've spent over a week dancing around what happened in the barn, neither of us willing to say a word about what happened. His blunt communication surprises me.

"What's your plan here, Lennon? Are you going to sleep with him?"

I look down at where my hand now rests on the game, tapping near the start button. "You're being inappropriate." It's my turn to lower my voice.

"Are you?" he presses, and when I look up at him again, I decide I won't back down.

The lie tastes bitter on my tongue. "Maybe."

"It won't be good." Noah steps closer, his nostrils flaring as he looks down at me.

"And how would you know?" I ask.

"That guy–" He flicks his head in Reece's direction. "He's not going to know how to handle you."

My brows lower, and I have the decency to be offended. Not know how to *handle* me? What the actual fuck? "And how am I supposed to be handled, Noah?" I practically spit the words at him.

Noah leans down, but I refuse to back away. At first, I'm relying on the spite that strengthens me, but when his lips brush my ear, my neck, I can't help the way my stomach flips.

My skin set aflame at his touch and the memory of his fingers inside me. I want him–his hands–his mouth.

It's pathetic.

"You know the sound you make when your orgasm finally starts building?" he starts. "That breathy little whine, you do?"

My heart pounds, the slickness between my thighs becoming all too apparent. "I–" I don't know how to respond. His body is so hot this close to mine, and I'm scared I might actually burn alive right here in this bar.

"I know it," he answers, his fingers ghosting over mine on the gaming console. "I crave hearing that sound from you because it means I'm doing my job."

"Your job?"

Noah's lips brush the shell of my ear, and I shudder. My entire body feels like a live wire.

"Tell him to go home, Lennon." He presses a kiss to my neck. "I love this skirt, by the way." He pinches the hem with his finger and thumb, placing another soft kiss on my sensitized skin. "Tell him to go home and save him the embarrassment."

I nearly close my eyes and give in, but I refuse to back down. He was a fucking asshole yesterday, and Noah Ashwood deserves to know it.

"No." I step back, holding my ground.

"Lennon–" he starts.

"I'll see you tomorrow, Noah. Nine sharp. We have furniture to pick out."

Without another word, I turn on my heel and find my way to the bar where Reece is finally grabbing a hold of two beers. I take mine, chugging as much as I can gulp down before setting it on the wooden bartop and looking him in the eyes.

"Let's go," I say.

"Go?"

"Yeah. I don't want to be here anymore. I'm leaving."

Reece looks confused, and rightfully so, but as my eyes fight the urge to find Noah across the crowded venue, I realize I don't care.

Because Noah was right–it wouldn't be good because Reece isn't *him*.

Twenty-Two

Noah

I have no rights to Lennon, but seeing her show up at the bar yesterday on a fucking date has driven me absolutely mad.

We aren't together and went so far as to agree upon those terms.

I stare at her house, car parked in the gravel driveway with my phone in my hand. She'd asked me to help her pick out furniture prior to whatever shit show happened yesterday, and despite the undercurrent of frustration, I couldn't help myself.

Me: Here.

I tilt my head against the back of the seat, my emotions a mess of threads I try to untangle.

Clear communication. That's what we'd discussed in my class Friday night, and that's what I'd attempted at the bar. Jealous and wanting, seeing her walk in that bar had me realizing how fucked up everything I felt was following my conversation with Alexis. I *wanted* Lennon–in whatever way she would have me.

So, when she exits the house, descending the porch wearing maroon leggings, an oversized sweater, and a beanie on her head, my chest tightens.

The door opens, and she climbs in with a soft smile on her pink lips. With cheeks slightly flushed from the cooler weather, she sighs, settling into the warmth of my vehicle.

"Hey," I start, dropping my phone in the cupholder next to my coffee cup. My resolve to communicate clearly crumbles, the fear of spooking her overpowering me. "You ready?" I ask.

Lennon looks at me, smiling wider. "Yeah," she answers before adjusting the beanie on her head. "Let's make this bitch the best bed-and-breakfast in the Midwest."

I chuckle, placing my hand on the back of her headrest to back out of her driveway.

• • • ● ● • ● ● • • •

"You think we'll have more luck here?" I ask, keeping my pace even with Lennon's as we near the store. The giant automatic revolving door greets us when we enter the blue building and walk toward the escalator.

The showroom stretches out on the second floor, exposed duct-work overhead making the entire space feel like a warehouse–which I suppose it is.

"Well, I hope so," Lennon answers. "It would be too time-con-suming to thrift *everything*." One boot steps off the escalator, and I follow her to the showroom. She looks like she's stepped out of an L.L. Bean catalog–like a cozy autumn hike that leaves you breathless when you finally reach the view you'd been looking for.

I, on the other hand, look as though I'm ready to teach a class with my dark academia-style sweater and dress pants. The pants, for what it's worth, are more casual.

It *is* the weekend, after all.

An arrow on the ground guides us between the individual sec-tions built to resemble real living spaces, and Lennon strides toward the first staged showroom, throwing herself onto a cream-colored cushion.

Crossing her legs, she beams up at me. "Think I need a new couch?" she asks as I sink into the spot beside her.

A smile dances on my lips. "Yours is quite small," I remark, noting the difference in size of the sofa.

"It's kind of a problem for guests, isn't it?" Lennon scrunches her nose, and my eyes trace over her freckles before meeting her gaze once more. She sighs, leaning her head back against the couch, and I do the same. "Plus, the living room is bigger in the house. I could add chairs, too. It just needs more seating." She blows out a breath and looks up at the ceiling. "Right now, it looks so empty."

I close my eyes, drumming my hands on my stomach. I can feel the warmth of her gaze when she turns to me, but I don't look.

It's eating me alive, not knowing where I stand with her–wanting her just the same. Remembering the way her breath hitched, her reddening cheeks, the way her bottom lip looked ready to devour has my body warming. Did she sleep with that guy? After what we did in the barn, I had assumed–

There's never been talk of us being anything but friends and casual. In fact, there hasn't been a lot of talk at all, and I'm itching to figure out what is going on in her head. I don't have rights to those details, though. And what if she *did* see us as something more than just friends?

I'm beginning to admit that I might want that, but could I pull it off? I fucked up around Julia, yesterday.

Fuck.

"What are you doing?" she asks, a soft laugh escaping her.

I turn my head to look at her and raise a brow, my head still resting on the plush cushion to our backs. "Too good for napping," I say. "You don't want guests falling asleep in communal spaces. It's rude."

I stand dramatically, making my way across the walkway to the next room over. "Now this," I say, throwing myself on the significantly smaller couch. Green velvet and wide cushions. It could work if she's purchasing chairs as well. And I'm sure the price tag would be nicer.

"Noah," Lennon says while standing over me. I want to drown in the way she says my name. "This isn't a sectional."

I move around a little to make my point. "Yeah, but look. The cushions are wide." I recall the detached way she introduced me to the guy yesterday, the way she refused to look at me. I test the waters. "You could spoon all night after watching unpopular movies with the guy you have mutual friends with."

Lennon doesn't flinch. She just raises a brow at me, still standing and refusing to join me. "I suppose that guy with mutual friends might consider fucking me on the couch and then fucking one of his colleagues on *her* couch a week later."

I'm certain the color drains from my face. "I didn't fuck her, and she isn't a colleague."

Lennon turns to sit next to me, but there's a clear distance between us. "Then who is she, if not a colleague?"

I know I should answer her—should end this before it begins, but I can't help it. Lennon enjoys her privacy, but I'm desperate to know what she's thinking—how she feels. "Would it matter who she was?" I ask.

"No." She spits her answer out so fast I barely catch it.

There's a quiet between us—six inches of space and plenty of unspoken words as I stare at her. "Would it matter, Lennon?" I ask again, feeling my heart like a drum behind my rib cage. "Would it matter if I told you I haven't been with anyone in weeks?"

She rolls her eyes. "You already said that yesterday during your tantrum."

"It's true." I risk leaning closer, the sweet scent of jasmine and amber surrounding me. "I can't fucking think about anyone else," I admit. My class would be proud. *Jane Austen* would be proud.

Lennon turns, our faces so close I can see each individual freckle dotting her nose–her cheeks. I want to trace them, connect the dots, and see if they'll unveil whatever she has running through her mind. Her lips part, making me aware of every breath that passes through them.

The giant warehouse shrinks down to just us–just the small space separating me from her. I lower my voice. "It's just you, Lennon."

"You tell that to all of them?" she asks, her voice a near whisper, her eyes searching.

I hold her gaze. "There's none of *them*. Not since you." Another breath, and I fight the urge to lean forward–press my mouth to hers and pull her bottom lip gently between my teeth. "You, on the other hand–"

"I left after the bar."

My brows shoot up.

"I couldn't sleep with him. I couldn't even be around him without thinking about what you said." She swallows, and I watch her throat, remembering how it felt to place my mouth there, to brush her skin with my thumb and listen to the small sound that snuck out. "I couldn't be with someone knowing I'd be thinking of you the entire time."

A thrill shoots down my spine at the thought. I want to pull her on top of me, feel the soft strands of her hair woven through my fingers and tug until my mouth lands on her neck, drawing sounds from her lips before kissing them away.

The reality of two screaming toddlers shocks me out of my thoughts.

Lennon sucks in a breath, looking out to the parts of the showroom we haven't seen. With the trance broken, she stands, moving toward another couch. "Whoa," she says, and I'm helpless to follow. "Look at this bathroom." Lennon smirks, tucking herself into the small shower. "It's so tiny."

With more walls, this part of the showroom hides us better, so I join her. My chest brushes her back when I stand amid the white tile. There's no way someone would want this damn thing. You couldn't even wash your ass.

I turn, noting every part of her body that touches mine. Heat blooms in those spots, warming my blood. "Hardly any room in here," I observe before leaning forward, trailing my nose up her neck until I'm whispering in her ear. "Bend over and see if I can–"

"Nope," Lennon walks away, but I don't miss the smile playing on her lips.

I catch up to her, and she turns to face me.

"We should probably quit stopping," she says. "I'm technically here to find storage." She waves her hands around. "Not all of this."

When her boots follow the arrows on the smooth concrete flooring, I follow her, my fingers brushing hers, just briefly. "You have some other place to be?" I ask, not really knowing how long she was planning to do this for.

"No," she answers before chewing on her bottom lip. "I just don't want to take up your whole day today."

My fingers twitch, brushing against hers again. "Lennon," I start, noting the way she doesn't pull away. We keep walking, and I let myself take her hand, weaving our fingers together. A smile stretches across my face when I look at her. "I want nothing more than to have all my days taken up by you."

• • • ● • ● • • •

Lennon picked out two bookshelves, and I'm thankful to have a project that doesn't require heavy research before beginning. The only issues I have are the confusing as shit pictures and the tiny ass tool they gave me to make it all work.

The good news is that Lennon put the other bookshelf together alongside me, so it's more of a team effort. It also gives me more time with her.

"You good, there?" I watch her concentrated expression as she places a nail and hesitates with the hammer.

"Don't be sexist." Lennon bangs the nail into the wood until it's fully seated before finally looking up with a satisfied smile on her face.

I focus on placing the back piece of the bookshelf, finding the nails and setting to work.

With a firm grip on the hammer, I swallow, not knowing how to bring up my next question. "So," I start between each bang of the hammer. The rhythm distracts from the vulnerability–the way

I'm showing all my cards at once. "You consider my offer about my family's Thanksgiving?"

Lennon misses, pulling her thumb between her lips and sucking. "Fuck," she whispers.

I gently wrap my fingers around her wrist, inspecting the spot where the hammer hit her. It's pink but doesn't look too bad.

She snatches her hand away. "You're being sexist." She smiles. "I can take a small pounding."

I laugh, sitting back onto the floor, as her smile breaks wider, white teeth flashing. "Yeah, okay," I say. I pick up my own hammer, keeping an eye on her as she finishes nailing the back of her own bookshelf to the wood. "You didn't answer my question. My family?"

She doesn't look at me, but the corners of her mouth remain pulled up–just slightly. "Yeah, sure. Only if you're willing to fly to Minnesota and protect me from all judgment."

I hear the sarcasm in her tone–the way she thinks I must be joking. I am not. "Yeah," I say. "I already agreed to that. Tell me when, and I'll get flights."

What has possessed me to meet Lennon's family? I have no idea. Maybe it's that I want to meet the asshole that is her father–maybe I just want to be in her world. Regardless, I will have time off as the college students head home for break, and I want her with me at my parent's house, too.

Something shifted while we were shopping today. I can still feel the warmth of her hand in mine, the press of her mouth to my cheek when I found the exact bookshelves we are working on.

I *want* to let her in. I don't want to be just friends, but I can't get myself to say it—not yet.

Lennon pauses, staring at me. "You don't really have to do that."

"I want to." We've both stopped building. "There's nothing I'd rather be doing with my Thanksgiving." When I offer a small smile, I realize just how true the statement feels. The idea of spending three days with her, seeing her childhood home? I can't think of anything more appealing.

"If you're serious."

"Oh, I'm completely serious."

We finish the bookshelves; the conversation diverting to at least ten other topics before we're done and staring at our handiwork placed strategically against the wall in the living room.

I adjust the watch on my wrist. "Planning on filling these with books about people fucking?"

Lennon smiles. "The guests will be so happy, they'll never want to leave. I'll be a raging success."

I laugh. "Yeah, but you may be the one wanting to leave. Hearing all that through the walls and the ceiling. It's unfortunate that your bedroom is on the bottom floor."

She runs a finger along the wooden shelf. "Not unfortunate if you ever come over to visit." Her cheeks turn pink as she refuses to look at me.

I feel the blood rush to my cock. "Yeah?" I ask, watching as she inspects the shelves. Her fingers run along the stained wood, and all I can think about is how it would feel to have her touch me—have her relieve this ache. "Why is that?"

Lennon turns, her eyes bright with desire. "I am really very good at being quiet, Noah." Her tongue peeks out to wet her bottom lip. "Like I said, I can take it."

My eyes linger on her mouth–utterly kissable–before returning to her green gaze. "You're good at being quiet?" There's a challenge in my question, followed by a brief pause–one charged with all the tension buzzing between us.

I can't help the memories of her flooding my mind–thinking about her in that damn skirt at the bar, wishing she'd worn it for me.

"Are you hungry?" she asks. "For lunch, I mean. I probably have something in the kitchen, and then we could play a game?"

I clear my throat. "Sure, yeah. That sounds good."

Lennon turns on her heel, walking away, and I can't help the way I stare at her as she goes–thinking about all the ways I could make her promise to keep quiet so utterly difficult.

Twenty-Three

Lennon

After lunch, I ended up picking cards out of the box in my bedroom closet. I didn't have it in me to go searching for any board games, so while it is not the most engaging choice, I decided on Go-Fish.

Noah leans against the back of the wooden chair in the dining room across from me. The bay window behind him faces away from the barn, revealing a stretch of grass before the line of trees. With the sun dipped below the horizon, deep purple paints the dark sky where stars will be peeking out at any moment. It's one of the reasons I love the place–secluded, but not so far out of the city it wouldn't make sense.

My small kitchen table from the apartment rests atop the original hardwood I fell for upon first sight. The table feels out of place–too simple next to the crown moulding. In a few months, when I get a bit more cash, I vow to furnish this room next. Pacing myself will ease the financial strain.

Which is a ridiculous thought because I'm already in enough debt, as it is. Nobody told me girlbossing involved financial ruin. It would have helped to know the truth.

"Is Go-Fish your favorite of the card games?" Noah looks at me over the cards in his hands, spread out like a fan. "Because, to be perfectly honest, this is a little slow."

He's not wrong.

"What if we change the rules? I don't know where I packed the other board games, so we are stuck with a deck of playing cards, but I'm sure we could figure something out how to make it more interesting."

Something darkens in his gaze, causing my stomach to swoop and dip like an acrobat. "I think I have an idea."

I lick my lips, his stare heating every part of me it touches, engulfing me in flames. The sensation sets every nerve ending alight, buzzing with need. "What's your idea?"

Noah leans forward, his sweater rolled to his elbows that are now planted firmly on the wooden tabletop. "Every time we draw a card, we also remove a layer."

"Of skin?" I say, knowing full well that's not what he meant. "Gross. Next, you're going to tell me you brought lotion for me to use."

Noah chuckles, that dimple popping in his cheek. "I meant clothes," he clarifies.

When his brown eyes hold mine, and I can't look away. There's a challenge there–one I'm willing to meet.

I pick my cards up off the table, swallowing. "Sure," I say as a thrill runs through me. After a day of picking out furniture, holding hands, and spending time together, what we're doing feels danger-ous.

Noah confessed to some form of exclusivity, and I'm not sure what it means, but it feels different. I have a feeling he doesn't operate that way with the other women he sleeps with. Plus, it's been weeks.

Weeks of laughing, banter, flirting, and splitting open every hope or dream that's taken up space in my heart for the last decade.

I feel known–seen in a way that makes me want to reveal more to him. For an English Professor, there's no judgment in Noah. I can't help but decide I'd be willing to let him pick me apart–analyze me like a classic piece of literature.

I'd be safe under his scrutiny.

I lick my lips. "Do you have any fives?"

He fights his widening smile, biting the inside of his cheek before he says exactly what I thought he would. "Go-Fish."

As if operating in slow motion, I draw a card and add it to my hand before placing my lot on the table. I pull the beanie off my head and run my fingers through my hair until I'm convinced the hat head is as good as it gets.

If my hair looks flatter than my chest in the seventh grade, Noah doesn't let it show.

Picking up my cards, I roll my tongue along my cheek. "The forehead doing it for you?" I ask, and Noah lets out a breathy chuckle.

"It really is."

I smile. "Your turn."

Tapping a finger on the wooden surface, he scans his cards before settling on a question. "Do you have any fours?" I look at my hand, hating the gift the universe gave me before handing the card over.

"Unfortunate," I say. "I was really looking forward to getting a glimpse of your ankles."

"How scandalous." He leans forward, the dimple deepening in his cheek. "I actually built my OnlyFans following by exclusively posting pictures of these ankles."

I throw my head back laughing, holding my cards to my chest. "And the universe decided I don't get to see them?" I question. "How much is a subscription?"

"For you?" Noah blows out a breath, his eyes lighted. "Free live shows every weekend, provided you offer me a job at the Inn."

"Showing ankle?" My heart squeezes in my chest, soaking up every ounce of charm he throws my way.

Noah pushes the glasses up his nose, cocking an eyebrow in my direction. "I'd love nothing more than to become an ankle stripper for your guests."

I chuckle, noting the two tens in my hand. "Tens?"

Noah shakes his head. "Go-Fish, Lennon."

My name rolling off his tongue sends a chill down my spine. I hold his gaze as I reach my hands under my sweater, unhooking the back clasp of my bra, and carefully reaching into my sleeves to remove the straps before dragging it out without revealing an inch of skin. I let it dangle by my finger and make a show of dropping it on the floor.

The chair creaks when Noah shifts, a low sound rumbling from his chest.

"Kings?" he asks, and I note the one in my hand–making a quick decision.

"Go-Fish," I say, knowing full well it's a fucking lie.

He doesn't waste time grabbing the back of his sweater and shedding the layer, leaving him in a white undershirt, his biceps pulling the hem of the sleeves taut. "Your turn."

I squeeze my thighs together, helpless to the pull of his shirt across his chest–his arms.

"Fives?" I cock an eyebrow, and Noah huffs a laugh.

"You already asked that," he says.

Feigning ignorance, I draw a card before standing up and pulling my leggings down. My sweater hits mid-thigh, keeping me covered. I hold the leggings out before letting them drop on the floor. His gaze follows every movement, heating when he catches sight of the thong falling to the ground in the heap.

He swallows just before I sit down on the chair.

"Do you have any twos?" he asks, his voice lower–sensual.

I don't bother picking up my cards. I place my elbows on the table, leaning forward as I hold steady eye contact. The air is as thick as my voice when I speak. "Go-fish, Noah."

"You didn't look."

"I said Go-Fish."

Noah pulls the white undershirt off, revealing the planes of his chest, his stomach, the dusting of hair that trails downward, and I let my eyes linger.

I lean back, my cards still stacked on the table. "I don't have it," I say.

Gathering up his cards, Noah sets them off to the side. "Pity. I thought we'd be better at this game."

"I think we are very good at it, actually." I tug at the sleeves of my sweater before pausing. "Care to help?"

Noah stands, slowly rounding the table and prowling toward me. I push away from the table, the scratch of the chair echoing as it grinds across the floor. When he stands in front of me, Noah reaches for the bottom of my sweater, thumbing the fabric before slipping both hands in.

The calluses on his palms scratch against the skin of my thighs. When his hands rise higher, thumbs brushing over my hip bones, I suck in a breath.

"You were right," I whisper.

"About?" he questions.

"Reece would never know how to handle me in this situation." I stand, Noah following my movements, pressing closer when I rise to my full height, his hands still under my sweater. My heart pounds when I let my hand run over the planes of his chest, feeling every dip and curve–the heat of his skin.

My voice drops to a whisper as he leans in, his lips so close they're almost touching mine.

He's everywhere all the time–fixing the house, in my dining room, in my head. I downloaded that dating app because I was a wreck. Noah doesn't *do* relationships, but what we're doing definitely toes the line. I want him.

I want him building bookshelves and watching movies–eating charcuterie late into the night. As he gently lifts the sweater higher, tugging until it's over my head, added to the lump of clothing on the floor, I struggle to catch my breath.

Noah presses his mouth to my shoulder, warm and wet, as I hold his biceps, needing some sort of anchor.

"I don't think anyone would know how to handle me," I admit, trailing one hand over his skin until my fingers are in his hair, tugging slightly. "You've ruined me for anyone else."

A dark sound leaves his mouth when he kisses me–devouring and needy.

His hands grip my ass, and I moan, tugging his bottom lip into my mouth, biting and soothing it with my tongue.

Noah groans, his hands lowering to the backs of my thighs as he lifts me, gently placing me on the dining room table before his tongue enters my mouth, tangling with mine.

I make a note to buy a new table sooner rather than later–especially when he presses forward, a hand slipping between my legs, his finger running along the seam of me.

"You're so fucking wet, Lennon."

I gasp, tilting my head when his mouth finds my neck, sending jolts of pleasure through my blood. I shift, encouraging him–begging him to touch me.

My hands move, memorizing every muscle beneath the stretch of his heated skin, the way his bicep flexes when he presses a finger into me.

His other hand finds my breast, thumb flicking over my nipple. Every breath–every touch feels intensified. It's as if I can't be anything but present with him in the moment–needy.

I whimper when his thumb circles my clit as he adds a second finger.

"I love the sounds you make." His mouth moves lower, sloppy kisses trailing downward until his tongue finds my nipple, his hand still working me as pleasure builds.

I'm drowning in him, my eyes squeezed shut, climbing to the peak of my orgasm, when I suddenly feel empty.

My eyes snap open, watching as Noah brings his fingers to his mouth, his lips parting around them, sucking until they're clean.

I squeeze my thighs together, reaching for the button of his pants. Noah gently grabs my wrist to halt my motions before pulling a condom out of his pocket, opening the foil with his teeth.

With his pants around his ankles, cock sheathed in the condom, Noah leans forward, heated and consuming. "I liked spending time with you today," he whispers against my mouth.

My chest feels full, warmth washing over me at his words. "I liked it, too." When the head of his cock presses against me, I moan, moving my hips in encouragement.

Noah brushes my hair away from my face, pausing as his warm brown eyes soak me in. I feel splayed out beneath him–fully myself and fully appreciated.

His fingers trail down the side of my face, sending sparks in their wake until his hand is around my throat–gentle and warm. He takes a deep breath before leaning down and pressing his lips to my neck, just above his hand. "You look so fucking good." Another kiss. "You always do."

I arch up, pleading for him to *take*. His praise has the temperature rising, my body squeezing around emptiness and leaving me desperate.

"I want to watch you come," he whispers, his thumb stroking my skin, nose trailing up until his lips are at my ear, biting–teasing. "I want to watch the flush bloom over your chest when you gasp my name."

He's still there, his cock brushing against me, refusing to fill me the way I want.

The hand at my throat migrates lower, over my chest, down to my breast as his hips press into me. It's not enough.

I wrap my legs around him, pulling him closer, and a tether seems to snap. Noah's breaths are harsh, wild as his forehead drops to mine. "Fuck, Lennon. *Fuck.*"

When he pushes into me, I cry out, my nails scratching down his back. He pulls back, filling me again, and a guttural sound pulls from deep in my throat.

"I thought you were going to be quiet?" he asks, his breathy chuckle driving me wild.

"Fuck that," I say before he pushes into me again. My body stretching around him, skin slick with sweat.

Noah chuckles again, and the warmth of his breath on my cheek has me moaning again. "Yeah, okay," he says, his hand is on my hip, holding me steady as he enters me. "Fuck that," he parrots. "I want to hear you scream."

His mouth lowers onto mine, swallowing his name when I cry out.

Twenty-Four

Noah

The hot steam of the shower clouds the mirror of my bathroom while I place a towel around my hips.

The faculty meeting we had ran later than I thought, and I'm scrambling to get ready before my parents' Thanksgiving dinner. Luckily, Lennon didn't mind changing plans and heading my way instead of having me pick her up.

The past few weeks have been a blur of home improvements, sex, long conversations, and more sex. Instead of curbing my appetite, every time I'm with her, I become more addicted. It's gone beyond just sleeping together, and part of that scares me.

You've ruined me for anyone else.

I run a hand down my face. "Fuck," I whisper.

As I dress for her arrival, I can't help but ponder how her meeting my family feels different. I don't bring women to meet my fucking family–haven't since Alexis.

When my mom found out, she immediately spiraled into planning an elaborate meal, complete with a newfound motivation for placing fall decor around the house. I tried to assure her that Lennon was just a friend, but something about that word felt inherently wrong.

Lennon's not just a friend.

Lennon's much more.

She's harsh truths and sarcastic jokes–cinnamon and hot cider.

I run my hands through my dark hair. Whether it's to look nice or calm my nerves, I don't know.

Either way, when the doorbell sounds, I jolt, running my palms over my black pants before adjusting the white collar of my shirt beneath the sweater I've chosen.

Giving myself one last glance, I head to the door, turning the handle and opening it until Lennon stands before me wearing the fucking skirt.

It's shorter–just above mid-thigh. Something about the sheer black tights, the black turtleneck sweater tucked into the thing–

She looks utterly fuckable.

"You need to change."

Lennon's brow furrows. "Wow, what an asshole." She shoves past me and makes her way to the living room before turning around. "Why? I thought you said you liked this?"

I reach for her, pulling her closer until her body is flush against mine. There's a lingering chill on her skin from the November air outside as I hold her close, my hands migrating to the bottom hem of the skirt. I slip one hand beneath it, noting the way she sucks in a breath.

"Noah," she warns. "We're going to be late."

"Fuck if I care." My hand rises higher, squeezing the outside of her thigh before migrating to her ass. *God,* she feels good in my hand.

My lips ghost over the skin of her neck, flushed and needy as I fight the urge to taste her.

"You're right," I say, drawing back and relishing in the soft whine that escapes her. "Don't want to keep my dad waiting. This is his favorite holiday."

• • • ● • ● ● • • •

A few stray leaves litter the walkway leading to my parents' greenhouse, the white railing lining the porch on my childhood home.

I'd stopped by two weeks ago to help Dad clean up the yard, raking and discussing the possibility of bringing Lennon to dinner. He'd gotten quiet—something I'm used to when I have conversations with my dad, but it wasn't until I saw his face that I noticed the change in his expression.

I reminded him she was only a friend. To which he responded with *sure* and proceeded to rake the leaves in the grass.

The front door sits closed as we amble up the steps, one old pumpkin drooping and looking sad near the top.

"My mom's going to freak about that." I nod toward the pumpkin, and Lennon offers a wide smile.

"Why?" she asks.

"I'm sure she's spent hours getting the house ready for your arrival. She loves having guests, especially if it means she gets to cook and play board games."

"Play board games?"

I chuckle. "I was an only child, remember? It's less fun with only two or three people. She gets very excited at the opportunity to create some real competition."

Lennon laughs, and the door swings open, my mom striding out in her long floral skirt flowing around her ankles and a sweater.

"Lennon," she says, warmth coating her voice. "It's so wonderful to meet you! It's been a long time since Noah brought a girl to the house."

My stomach drops. "Mom."

She waves me off. "Come in, come in. I'm making tons of food, and I was thinking we could play Life. Or maybe we could play Clue instead."

"Clue would be better," I chime in, but she seems to ignore me as she drags Lennon into the entryway, taking her jacket and ushering her toward the kitchen.

Lennon looks back at me as she slowly disappears down the hall. Her smile is bright as the sun, and I can do nothing but unwind the scarf around my neck, drop my peacoat over the banister, and follow her light.

"I was actually thinking about purchasing new cookware for the bed-and-breakfast." I hear Lennon say as I enter the kitchen. My mom stands near the stove, glancing over at her as she speaks. "Well, it's more of a need. I can't keep cooking on what I bought right out of college."

My mom chuckles. "You let me know what you need. We'd be happy to gift some things." Her eyes flick to me. "Noah, here, says he's been helping with renovations. I've yet to reap the rewards of this, though. Our finished attic still has a hole in the wall from last spring when squirrels made a nest there." She waves a hand. "Terrifying when the thing chewed through the plaster and got out. Anyway, Joel covered it with a piece of wood, and it looks hideous. Noah could have had it fixed by now with all his new skills."

Lennon leans against the countertop, her hands gripping the marble as she stares me down, one long leg crossed over the other at the ankle. "Yeah, Noah? Why haven't you fixed it yet."

I lean over the kitchen island, holding her gaze. "Five minutes, and you've turned against me."

Lennon raises a brow, my mom humming while she works over the stove. "I actually prefer being up against you."

I nearly choke as my dad walks in from the side door carrying a grocery bag. "I bought the rolls, but I'm not sure why–"

My mom smacks him in the chest with a spoon and shushes him before turning and smiling sweetly at Lennon. "Lennon, dear. All of my food is homemade."

"Don't let her lie to you," my dad says, holding up the rolls. "She has me out here running around town doing her bidding." He kisses my mom on the forehead and sets the bag on the counter.

"Heard a lot about you," he admits, and Lennon smiles.

"Have you?" she asks. "What have you heard?"

"That Noah's been fixing up that house of yours."

"Joel, I just said that," my mom chimes in.

My dad wads up the grocery bag and throws it under the sink. "Must be pretty special to get him to learn how to replace wooden boards on a porch."

My face feels hot. My parents sound like they're talking to my girl-friend—someone I'm in a relationship with. Lennon and I haven't had any real conversation, but it doesn't seem wrong.

There's still a thread of anxiety in the back of my mind, warning me of all the ways things could go south with Lennon. My track record isn't great.

"Dad—" I say, but Lennon only smiles at him.

"Good to know I've helped him acquire some useful skills." She taps the counter once. "Um, where is your restroom?" she asks, and my mom points her down the hallway just before Lennon disappears.

"I like her, Noah," my mom says as soon as she's gone. "Far prettier than the last one. In the face, particularly."

"Mom, I'm not dating this woman," I say, and she rounds on me, her eyes blazing.

"Then that," she says, pointing her spoon in my direction, "is something you must remedy straight away."

I look to my dad for some sense of reprieve, but he merely holds his hands up in defense. "Don't look at me, Son," he says. "Your mother makes the rules here."

Twenty-Five

Lennon

Walking back through the hallway that leads to the kitchen, I stop to note the different pictures on the wall. Family photos of Noah and his parents, other people I don't know.

For a moment, I wonder if I'll see Alexis in one of the pictures, but I imagine his parents wouldn't do that. From what Noah told me, his family didn't even like her much. I'd assume cheating on him earned her the privilege of having all photos of her burned out back in a massive bonfire.

Loud singing echoes through the hall, and I continue on, entering the kitchen to find Noah holding a spoon in front of his face like a microphone and singing loudly with his mother. It's some old school rock song I'm unfamiliar with. But even if I knew it, I'm afraid Noah's singing is so bad the tune would be unidentifiable.

Noah spots me, rounding the kitchen island and grabbing my hand. "Dance with me," he says, before spinning me once. I laugh, humoring him.

When I'm facing him again, he has a wide smile plastered to his face. "You are actually terrible," I say.

"At dancing?" he questions.

I chuckle. "I was referring to the singing. Jury is still out on the dancing."

He kisses me on the cheek, and my face warms, knowing full well that his parents are right there watching. The affection feels easy–simple. But most of all, it feels like a relationship that Noah and I aren't in.

I clear my throat, looking down toward my black boots.

His mom tosses a spoon in the sink before spinning. "Food's ready," she announces.

My stomach twists in knots. It's not that I'm upset: it's that it feels so natural– like something I *could* want. I have had on and off again relationships, a few dates here and there since I graduated, but nothing serious.

Whatever I have with Noah feels like the most serious thing I've had since high school.

And the unfortunate fact is that it's not even a *thing* to begin with.

· · · ● ● ● ● · ·

I currently have four children and have taken on the role of soccer mom in the most literal sense of the word.

The good news is that I don't actually have to feed these fake kids.

The bad news is I'm pretty sure I lost one of the dumb fucking pink rods on the floor because it's so difficult to get them into the mini car that I'm moving around the game board.

My fifth child gets added to the lot.

"I think I'm at capacity with the number of things I can keep alive at this point." I wait for Noah's mom to take her turn.

Noah grins in my direction, his hand slipping beneath the dining room table and squeezing my thigh just below the hem of my skirt.

His mom chuckles. "Noah always talked about wanting children," she starts. "Is that something you want outside of board games?" My stomach churns.

Sure, I've thought about kids. It's not like I hated having Ellis's niece at the house, but the conversation feels–*intense*.

"Mom," he says, the smile falling from his face. For what it's worth, Noah looks as panicked as I feel. I just imagined the first time we had this conversation, we'd be having it in private.

Had I imagined this conversation?

He clears his throat, withdrawing his hand from its comfortable spot on my leg. "You don't have to answer that," he says without making eye contact.

His mom ignores him, looking at me expectantly. "I–" Shifting in my seat, I can feel my face heating. "I do, eventually. I'm working on the bed-and-breakfast though–getting the business up and started, but someday." Offering a small smile, I glance at my game piece on the board. "Maybe not a whole van full, but–"

"And what about marriage?" she presses. His mom looks down, moving her own car over spaces and treating this like some sort of casual conversation–like we're not talking about the future and marriage and kids.

"Mom!" He stands, holding his hand out to me, and I take it. "Will you excuse us for a moment?"

"Sure, sweetie." His mom smiles as if she didn't just ask her son's female friend that he frequently sleeps with if she wants marriage and kids.

Noah pulls me down the hallway and up the stairs, opening the door to one of the rooms and ushering me inside.

There's a shelf littered with soccer trophies above the full-sized bed, a hideous blue color smeared on the walls, and a bookshelf riddled with unholy amounts of middle-grade fiction. I'm surprised the thing hasn't collapsed at the weight of it.

My face is hot, but I reach for the joke anyway. It's far more comfortable than talking about anything real. "Quite scandalous," I quip. "What are they going to think we are doing up here?"

"Probably making one of your many children," he says, and I frown.

Noah's smirk falls in response. "Look," he says, stepping closer. "I'm sorry about that. I told her you were here as a friend, but I don't know if she was listening. Or maybe she's just confused. I don't really bring women home, so they're probably misinterpreting what's happening between us. I don't want my mom to freak you out, and family is important to her. I just–"

"What–" I tilt my head to the side, starting again. "What *is* happening between us?" I ask, my voice quieter than I'd like. I sound small–insecure.

And maybe I am. Before the last ten minutes, we'd had a great time dancing in the kitchen, eating ridiculous amounts of food, and chatting. I felt comfortable. Noah's been free with affection, stealing a kiss on the cheek or grabbing my hand under the table during dinner. Maybe his mom has a right to be confused. I sure am.

"We're friends," he says, and it feels like a knife to the stomach.

"Yeah," I say, somewhat irritated and trying my best to hide it. "We established that." I clear my throat, smoothing my hands over my skirt. "We are friends who aren't allowed to go on dates with other people, apparently."

Noah pauses. He's standing a mere three feet away from me, but he feels so much farther. "I never said you weren't allowed. I just didn't enjoy seeing it."

The irritation breaks through. I'm helpless to stop it. "Noah," I say, "you showed up and practically scared the last guy off. In fact, that's the second date of mine you've ruined. You started talking about sex." I'm talking with my hands, becoming more pissed off the more I speak. "Which we have had, by the way. Multiple times. Too many times to count as friends. You said a lot of things at the furniture store that led me to believe none of the things you're saying right now align with your true feelings."

"I know. I'm sorry," he says, blowing out a breath. Noah steps closer. "Listen, I know you aren't looking for any kind of relationship with me."

My heart is pounding in my ears–so loud I'm afraid he might hear it from where he's standing. "I never said that," I say–admit. There's no sense in lying at this point. I'm in too deep, anyway. It's about time we started talking about it–about time I stop ignoring the very obvious feelings I have for him.

Fucking hell.

"I–" I can't get the words out. "I just mean, I know how you operate. I wouldn't ask for–"

Noah's brow furrows, and he looks offended. "How I operate?"

I huff a laugh, trying to ease some of the tension. "You're not interested in a relationship, Noah. You went on about why you bought a one-bedroom house. About as subtle as a gun, really. I'm just–I don't really know what I'm doing with you." Falling, probably. "And yeah. I do want children, I guess. Someday down the line, I'd like a lot of things, but with this," I gesture to him. "I suppose I'm just along for the ride. Going along with however you want to do things because I can't seem to stop spending time with you, and I *want* you, but that's not an option."

"You want me?"

I can't say it again. I'm usually so confident–not thinking about the consequences. Noah rejected me once. He refused to kiss me, but somehow, if he rejects me now, it feels like it'll actually mean something. It will cut deep, and I'm not sure I'll know how to stop the bleeding. "I–" My voice sounds quiet as the words get stuck in my throat.

Noah steps forward, placing his hands on my shoulders. His eyes are intense as he speaks. "I'm not *operating* in any kind of way. This isn't how I do things at all."

"What does that even mean?"

One hand comes up to cup my cheek as he leans in slowly, testing before he makes a move. I don't back away, and his lips gently brush against mine before I sink into him.

His hands thread through my hair as he deepens the kiss, adding pressure until my entire body feels hot.

When he pulls away, his lips hovering just above mine, he whispers, "I don't want you going out with other guys." It sounds like a confession. "I want you all to myself."

"As a friend."

His forehead presses against mine. "I don't know." When his voice drops, I fight the urge to lean into him. "I mean, I *do* know. I just don't want to spook you. I'm fine being friends if that's what you want."

One corner of my mouth turns up, my heart still pounding. "If we're just friends, our friendship sure has a unique quality to it." I chuckle. "I don't really act like this with Ellis or Cass."

Noah's laugh is low–pulled from somewhere deep in his chest. "So, you're telling me I'm special?" he asks.

"Yeah," I say.

Silence stretches between us for a brief moment, and I can almost hear the way his thoughts are spinning. I hope–*God do I hope*–that whatever he says next won't absolutely wreck me.

"What if–" he starts, sounding somewhat off balance. "What if we tried this for real, then? A relationship. Low pressure."

My hand tightens on his sweater as I pull him closer. "I think I'd like that."

"Yeah?" He sounds hopeful.

I press a kiss to the corner of his mouth, his jaw, and move downward to his neck. Heat washes over me at his nearness.

Slowly, I lower myself to my knees, staring up at him and noting the way his breaths have quickened, his mouth parted and hungry.

"What are you doing?" he asks as I trail my hands up his thighs, my fingers finding the button to his pants.

I smirk. "Establishing that we aren't friends."

Noah groans, and I release the button before dragging his zipper down slowly. I pull his briefs down, revealing his cock and stroking it with my hand. Once, twice–

Noah hisses. "Lennon, we're literally in my childhood room."

I arch an eyebrow at him. "You win all those soccer trophies?"

The blue walls surround us, not a single item out of place aside from the books thrown on the shelf. It's so *Noah*. The trophies lining the shelf give me a glimpse into his past along with the photo of a young Noah in a soccer uniform, smiling widely for the the camera.

I look away.

His hips thrust forward, urging me to keep stroking him with my hand. "Yeah," he grinds out, and I can already feel the wetness gathering between my thighs.

I lick my lips, loving the way he's slowly unraveling, losing control in the palm of my hand. My chest swells with the thought of doing this with him—surrounding myself with all the pieces of his history until I can make up for all the moments I *haven't* gotten to be in his presence.

Past, present, and future, I'm sure of one thing, I *like* him—so much.

When my mouth parts around his hardened flesh, stretching to accommodate his size, he groans again, and I can feel the sound everywhere.

Noah's hands are in my hair, gentle and guiding as I move, adding pressure with my tongue with every drag of his cock.

I glide my hand over him in time with my mouth, looking up as he stares at me, his hand tightening in my hair.

"You're so beautiful," he says, and I hum my approval. "*Shit.*"

I work him until he's panting, thrusting, and practically begging for release.

When I feel the warmth fill my mouth, I swallow it down greedily before standing and brushing my thumb over my lips.

"Noah?"

His dad's voice echoes from the hallway, and I quickly step away, laughing.

"We better go back down there," I say.

Noah presses a bruising kiss to my lips. "Come over tonight," he says. "I want to return the favor."

I smirk, straightening my hair before opening his bedroom door. "Sure. But only if you're willing to change the lightbulb in the kitchen for me."

Twenty-Six

Noah

The best part about Lennon's kitchen cabinets is that the hardware is not covered in paint. I had little home renovation experience before this, but I'm happy to say that I skipped the *bad landlord* stage of the process.

The hardwood creaks behind me, and I turn around to find Lennon standing there in leggings and an oversized sweatshirt. Her Christmas-themed socks poke out from inside her winter boots, and I chuckle. "A little early for Santa socks, don't you think?"

Lennon frowns. "By the time I finished my laundry, I didn't feel like matching all the socks. These, for very obvious reasons, were already matched and in the drawer."

My smile widens. "I'm sure nobody on the plane will even notice," I say, my smile widening. I nod toward the cabinets, their new, dark green color contrasting with the white tiled backsplash. "It looks good," I point out.

Lennon steps forward, wrapping her arms around my waist, and I pull her closer. "Yeah, I had some help." She smirks, her green eyes bright as she looks up at me. "I've been sleeping with some guy in exchange for favors."

I fake disgust before pulling her into my chest, my arms firmly wrapped around her shoulders. "Some guy is getting his hands on my girl?" I say. "How dare he."

My girl.

My chest tightens. When I broke things off with Alexis, I had decided that I wasn't cut out for relationships. I've been running ever since–throwing myself into frivolous encounters and my job. But after seeing Lennon in my parents' house, watching how she fit in with this *thing* I'd imagined but given up on–

"He's really quite good at what he does." Lennon scoots backward to lift herself up onto the counter, pulling me forward until I stand between her legs.

"Yeah?" I ask, leaning forward, my lips just inches from hers.

She tugs at the collar of my sweatshirt, pulling me in until her lips meet mine. Her kiss is leisurely–exploring as if we have the rest of our lives to taste each other.

My hands tug at her hips, pulling her into me as my tongue traces the seam of her mouth. She whimpers, her hands tugging at my hair, my jeans–anything to get closer.

I break the kiss. "We're going to miss our flight," I say.

"You nervous?" Lennon tilts her head to the side, one corner of her mouth turned up.

"Are *you?*" I ask.

She lets out a breath. "Yeah, actually." Groaning, she hops off the counter. "Plus, Griffin is out of town, so Ellis is all sad even though she doesn't want to admit it. I had ice cream delivered to her house last night when she was doing her weird complaining without really complaining thing."

I chuckle. "Can't she just hang out with Cass?"

"Well, yeah. But I'm a fucking catch. I don't blame her for being sad in the absence of my presence."

I kiss her temple before walking down the hall and picking up her bags at the door. Lennon follows. "You're right," I toss over my shoulder as we descend the very sturdy porch steps. "You *are* a catch."

● ● ● ● ● ● ● ● ● ●

Lennon's childhood home is much larger than I originally expected. The manicured lawn is apparent even through the dreary late fall season, and it matches the other houses on the street in a way that makes me positive these people are part of an HOA.

Based on what I know about Lennon's father, I wouldn't be surprised if he's the president.

"Shit your pants yet?" Lennon asks, and I laugh.

"Not even a little." I loop my hand through hers as we walk down the path to the house, our rental car parked in the driveway.

The mudroom is silent when we enter, the only sound is the blare of the television from a room over. When we follow the noise to the living room, nearly spotless save for the blond guy on the couch.

"Devon," Lennon says, and he turns, a wide smile on his face.

"There she is! Thought you weren't coming this year." Devon stands, wrapping Lennon in a hug before his brown eyes flick to mine.

She pulls away, somewhat stiff. "I tried to get out of it." When Lennon turns, she smirks, her shoulders visibly relaxing while Devon holds a hand out. "This is Noah," she supplies.

"Lorelei said you were bringing a friend." We clasp hands, shaking before separating. "Nice to meet you."

"Boyfriend, actually," Lennon corrects, and I can't say I don't like the word on her lips. I like it too much, in fact.

"Lennon's given me the rundown on everyone. You're married to her sister?" I glance around the room, noting the lack of family photos on the walls. In fact, the interior of the house matches the exterior. Somewhat cold, very much ready to be on the market at the drop of a hat.

It's strange that Lennon said she spent her whole childhood in this house.

Someone walks in from behind us, and by her facial features alone, I can tell it's Lennon's sister. Lennon's smattering of freckles are absent, but the red hair and bowed mouth give her away.

"You must be Noah!" she says, reaching out for a handshake. If I didn't know any better, I'd think I was making some kind of business deal with these people.

"That's me," I say, and Lorelei tucks herself under Devon's arm.

"Well, what do you know?" she starts, glancing between Lennon and me. "It turns out the English Professor traveling to meet the entire family in Minneapolis isn't *wildly out of the realm of possibilities.*"

"Things change," Lennon offers before looking back toward the door. "We should probably get our bags."

When she turns, I follow Lennon until we walk out the door and into the brisk air. Popping the trunk to the rental car, I grab both her suitcase and mine. "Not so bad," I say, before slamming the trunk closed.

Lennon leans against the side of the car. "*Those* aren't the people who raise my blood pressure."

I step closer, both bags in hand, as I peer down into her eyes, searching for an ounce of the confidence I usually find there. I don't want to see her light dimmed. "I bet I could raise your blood pressure if you gave me a chance."

Lennon laughs, planting a kiss on my lips before retreating toward the house. "You *are* infuriating."

"That's not what I was talking about."

When we re-enter, her mom is waiting in the mudroom to greet us, followed by Lennon's father. I can't help the way I'm judging everything about the guy. After hearing him on the phone–learning the things he's said to Lennon, I find it hard to like him.

The button-up he wears sits smooth over his chest, starched and pressed so that no wrinkles remain. There's nothing particularly warm about Mr. Yarrow, and I hate it.

"Lennon," he says, and his tone sounds official–business-like.

"Dad, this is Noah. Noah, Dad. Glad that part is done." Her body is rigid next to mine, and I hate the way it makes me feel. I reach for her hand, and despite it all, she takes it. Her dad's eyes flick to our interlocked fingers.

"I thought you said you were bringing a friend?" he asks.

"Boyfriend," Lennon corrects.

Her dad grunts, his lips pressing together in a thin line. "Pretty recent, I suppose." He turns toward me, his cropped hair graying beneath the harsh lights of the mudroom. What fucking lightbulbs do they use in this house? "You like football, Noah?"

"Not particularly."

Lennon tries to hold in a laugh, and it eases something inside me. "He's more of a soccer guy," she interjects.

Lennon's dad places a hand on my shoulder, squeezing harder than necessary. "No worries," he says. "Why don't you come and watch some football with us while the girls catch up."

Twenty-Seven

Lennon

“That wasn't so bad.”

Noah closes the door behind us as I throw myself on the bed, staring at the ceiling of my childhood room and wishing I had taken down the Jonas Brothers poster plastered to the wall near the bathroom that connects with my sister's room.

“Yeah, minus the part where you had to watch hours of football.”

“Not my favorite thing, but I'll survive.” The mattress sinks, and Noah sits next to me, staring at the very poster I've suddenly become embarrassed about.

"That poster seen a lot of action?" he asks, the amusement clear in his tone.

I smack him on the arm gently. "I didn't kiss posters in high school, if that's what you're implying." I smile. "Kind of weird that's where your mind went, Noah. Have a confession?"

"I'm not ashamed of my weird adolescent behaviors."

I snort a laugh, my legs still hanging off the bed as I melt further into the mattress, thankful that the introductions are over. Releasing a breath, the tension leaves my muscles, allowing me to truly relax for the first time all day.

Having Noah come to my family's Thanksgiving was not on my radar the last time I talked to Lorelei. I'm pretty sure she thought I was lying after I assured her he wouldn't be here, and then here he is, dating me, no less.

The consistency showcases the very best of my qualities.

Noah lays down beside me, his fingers intertwining with mine. For a moment, it's silent, and I can finally breathe.

I close my eyes briefly. "Ellis invited Cass to dinner with her family for tomorrow."

Noah turns his head to look at me. "Cass doesn't have family in the area?"

"I guess not. I feel bad I didn't invite her or something." My brow furrows. "An oversight, really."

"Third-wheeling in a different state sounds like a perfect holiday to me." Noah's smile is bright when I turn to look at him.

"Don't be such an asshole."

That dimple appears on his cheek just before he sits up, propping himself on his elbow. Noah places a hand on the side of my face, leaning in slowly as his thumb strokes my cheek. He smells like whatever cologne he's worn since the day we met, and I make a note to ask him what it is, if only so I can huff the bottle when he's not around.

"I'm glad you invited me, Lennon." His voice is low, intimate, as his lips hover an inch in front of mine.

"Not regretting it?" I ask, hating the thread of vulnerability in my voice.

"Not in the slightest." The press of his lips has me melting into him, pulling him closer until my whole world is taken up by Noah Ashwood.

I was certain he'd regret coming, and that he doesn't, sends a different kind of warmth through my body. Even when I'm an absolute dick to the guy, he's still in my corner—a steady presence that believes in me, in what I'm doing. He wouldn't have been painting those fucking cabinets last week if he didn't.

Plus, he reminds me pretty frequently.

Noah's hand migrates lower, skimming against my neck, and down until his finger brushes over my nipple. The soft bite to my lip has me moaning into his mouth, my body already buzzing with need.

When he shifts, hovering on top of me, I wrap my legs around him to draw him closer. The press of his cock against me driving me wild.

"Noah," I breathe.

"Think you'll be better about keeping quiet this time??" he asks through a breathy chuckle before grinding against me.

I gasp, leaning into his touch as he explores. "I think we should test it."

Noah shakes his head. "I want your dad to think I'm a respectful boyfriend."

"I'm sure he does." I arch into him, desperate for more contact. I'm not sure why he's still wearing clothes at this point.

His eyes darken as he looks down at me, but there's a softness there—something more. "He won't if he hears what I'm about to do to you."

His mouth is on mine, fingers fumbling with the hem of my sweatshirt, pulling and tugging until we are both bare and sprawled out on the bed.

Noah holds himself over me, lining himself up. I moan, trying to pull him closer, but he won't move.

"Noah," I practically beg, and he skims his lips over my neck, kissing my jaw as one hand squeezes my thigh.

"Condom," he murmurs, and I hate everything about it. All of it. I want *him*.

"I'm technically on birth control," I whisper, and he pulls back. His eyes searching. "Tested and clean. You?"

"I'm clean," he says.

I can still feel him there. "Please." My nails scrape gently down his back as his eyes darken, and he pushes in.

"Fuck," he whispers.

My hands are in his hair, tugging as my mouth explores any piece of skin I can get to, his thrusts keeping time with the beat of my heart. I lift my hips, grinding against him and feeling a spike of pleasure as my orgasm builds.

The room fills with harsh breaths, and when he whispers my name, I feel myself tip over the edge.

Noah's thrusts become erratic, chasing his own release. "I–"

He doesn't complete his sentence, groaning as he spills inside me.

Night has fallen outside the window, a few stars peeking out despite the streetlights in the neighborhood.

When we're done, Noah pulls me into him; His body curved around mine, and his arms wrapped around my torso.

There's no uncertainty–no question about what we are or what we're doing–just the gentle rise and fall of his chest at my back and the steady beat of my heart matching his rhythm to my own.

Twenty-Eight

Lennon

The first half of Thanksgiving day proved to be far better than I expected.

My mom is suddenly very fond of Noah because he chose to help her cook, though I'm not sure if it was something he was truly interested in, or if he just wanted to impress her.

As for my father, Noah seemed to charm him, too. Playing a game of basketball out in the driveway, and narrowly missing our rental car multiple times.

I'm thankful we got the extra insurance.

"I'd like you to know, I played a large role in preparing this Thanksgiving meal," Noah says as he sidles up beside me, wrapping an arm around my waist and pulling me to his side. "Emphasis on large."

I fight the smile that threatens to break free. "Are we still talking about your cooking skills?"

He laughs, the sound warming my chest. "Absolutely not."

"Well," my mom starts, popping her head into the living room. "Everything is set up. We might as well eat."

I look at Noah, brows raised. "Might as well," I repeat as we make our way into the dining room.

Pleasant conversation fills the space, and for a moment, I almost think we are going to get away with a nice trip. Noah's presence grounds me as my dad talks about his business endeavors, complimenting Lorelei on the new award she earned at work.

"So," my dad starts, poking at the stuffing on his plate. "How long have you and Noah been dating?" he asks, and I straighten in my chair.

Noah catches the shift—the way my emotions seem to shut off, and he grabs the leg of my chair, dragging it across the floor until I'm even closer to where he's sitting. It thaws some of the icy tension I'm feeling—just slightly.

"Officially?" I question, cutting into a piece of ham with the side of my fork. "It's fairly new."

Noah takes a sip of water, placing an arm around the back of my chair. "I've been helping out with the bed-and-breakfast," he says, inserting himself into the conversation. "Well, I've been helping with the renovations. Things are looking really great."

"Oh," my dad says, somewhat surprised. "Do you work in contracting?"

"He's an English professor," I say before taking a bite full of food.

My mom sits quietly at the other end of the table while Devon and Lorelei chat in their own personal bubble.

"You're not a contractor?" My dad's brows furrow as all of his attention shifts to Noah. I hate when he does that. Something about having Ian Yarrow's undivided attention draws up unpleasant feelings. It puts me on guard, and if that's happening with Noah, he doesn't show it.

"I'm not," Noah confirms.

"But you have experience with renovations?"

"I don't."

My father hums, the sound leaking judgment as he looks back down at his meal.

"The internet is a great educational resource," Noah jokes. "I have since graduated from Google University after learning how to fix a toilet with at least three separate videos."

I chuckle, and so does Mom, but my dad remains stoic—unamused.

My food sits like lead in my stomach when my dad's sharp gaze flicks to me. "I am not sure how you can have a serious business if you're relying on your boyfriend to get most of this work done, Lennon."

I brush it off, shutting down the racing thoughts in my head. The best way to handle feelings of inadequacy is to pretend they don't exist. My dad was *just* complimenting Lorelei on her reward, and now he's critiquing my business over dinner.

I can't say I'm surprised.

"To be fair," I start. "He wasn't my boyfriend when he started helping."

"Then how did you convince him to become your contractor?" My dad laughs, but the sound is hollow–filled with all the emptiness of whatever he wanted me to become–the thing I didn't achieve.

"I–"

Noah speaks up, his arm still around the back of my chair, his thumb brushing over my shoulder. "Painted the cabinets in the kitchen last week. They're looking really good. Lennon has talked about making the farmhouse feel cozy–really providing a unique experience with guests."

I lean back into him, thankful for the intercession.

"Huh?" My dad starts. "I really think you could have found a house elsewhere. Ohio doesn't seem like the state people go to have *unique* experiences. A larger tourist destination would have brought in more capital–proven you were really serious about this business supporting your financial goals."

Fuck if he knows anything about my *financial goals.*

"I am serious. And Ohio is fine." I can feel the walls closing in, suffocating any part of myself–my core that remains. If I can't change the way he sees me–if everything I've done isn't proof enough, then I might as well be whatever it is he's picturing.

"I hear Ohio is getting a lot of attention," Noah chimes in, his tone lighthearted–directly contrasting the feel of the room. "Kid's slang terms are really making the place a popular destination for all."

"That's not a reason to open a bed-and-breakfast there."

My mom, for what it's worth, rolls her eyes. Leaning toward Lorelei to say something I don't quite catch.

I can see the crease form between Noah's brows as if he's trying to find the right button to push to switch my dad's distaste for approval. Unfortunately for him, I know that button doesn't exist.

"Personally," Noah starts. "I've seen everything she's poured into this. I'm looking forward to seeing the business's success."

Devon chimes in, and I hate how childish it makes me feel. He's been around for a long while–knows too much. So much, that I sometimes feel like I'm under a microscope when I'm here.

"Lennon's never been known for pouring herself into much of anything." He laughs, and the sound stings. "Did you know she failed algebra two her sophomore year of high school? Didn't like the teacher, so she didn't apply herself."

My family chuckles like Devon has made an appropriate joke–one that doesn't tear me down to get a laugh. Or maybe that's the part that makes it funny. I don't know.

Noah doesn't balk at the challenge. "Seems like a good enough reason to me. I teach college students for a living. I'm sure they'd fail, too, if I wasn't engaging enough. It's an important part of the job."

"It was selfish," my dad says, and I tense at the word, hating the way it slices through me like a knife. "Destroyed her GPA right before her junior year. One of the reasons, I believe, she didn't get into the school where Lorelei attended." I shrink back because it's true. I did fail and got the college rejection. It would have been nice to have some empathy, but I've long since passed the hope of that from my father. "Had to go to the middle of nowhere Ohio for a business degree."

"Ian, that's enough." My mom's voice chimes in from the other side of the table as I take another bite of food. There's no sense in arguing. I'm just hoping the silence will trigger a shift in topic.

Noah, apparently, doesn't feel the same. "Pretty shitty to heavily critique your own daughter at the dinner table during a holiday, isn't it?" His tone has hardened, and I hate it because I see them turning him into the monster they created in me. "Especially in front of her boyfriend."

"How long have you been around again?" my dad asks, rising to the challenge. "She hasn't entertained anyone for very long."

Noah almost stands, his chair screeching across the floor before I grab his hand, forcing him to remain seated.

My dad scoffs. "Keeping real winners around, Lennon."

The table is quiet, nobody moving as I stare down the barrel of my father's gun.

Whatever he says, no matter how small, seems to hurt worse. I've always thought of myself as someone with thick skin, but here?

"Not that you'd care about me and my frivolous dreams," I mutter as my fork scratches across my plate.

"You'll grow out of it."

My anger swells, rising until I feel like I'm about to erupt. "I bought an entire house on my own at twenty-six. I've managed to figure out the business side of things. We should open next summer."

"And you're using your inexperienced boyfriend as a contractor. Honestly, Son, how much was she even paying you before you started dating?"

It's my turn to stand. "Not paying him," I say, my entire body shaking. "I just have to fuck him, and he helps paint some cabinets."

I don't turn around and walk out of the dining room to run up the stairs. Noah following after.

Twenty-Nine

Noah

I take the steps two at a time, following Lennon into the bedroom and closing the door.

"Lennon," I say, but she turns on me.

"You couldn't have just left it?"

I reel back. I understand why she's pissed. Her father is an asshole and doesn't believe in anything she's doing. I just watched her family sit idle while he tore her down—and the husband?

Fucking piece of work.

What I didn't expect was for Lennon to turn this on me. "What are you even talking about right now?" I step forward, but she moves back, her face twisted into a look of disgust.

"I don't need your help, Noah. If you knew how to shut up, he would have stopped."

The words fly through the air, sharp like blades as they hit their mark. If it wasn't bad enough that Lennon claimed to be fucking me for favors in front of her family, this really brings it all home.

"You were just letting him talk like that. I've never seen you take shit sitting down. And now you're yelling at *me*? What the actual fuck, Lennon?"

She's pacing, tension pulling every muscle in her body tight as she refuses to look at me. "You don't get to say that. How long have you even known me?"

"For the better part of a year."

Lennon stops, facing me fully, green eyes blazing. "Exactly. We ended up in this same position last spring–shouting on a patio because you have some weird obsession with protecting me. I don't need you to intercede on my behalf, thanks, Noah." She scoffs, continuing her pacing.

The way my voice rises makes my entire mouth taste bitter. "God, who even are you right now? You're the one who just announced to your entire family that you were fucking me for favors, and now you're telling me I shouldn't have stood up for you?"

She stumbles a step before turning and sitting on the bed. "You're right." She leans back, staring at the ceiling. "I feel off balance. I didn't think this through. It was a mistake bringing you here. You're not used to this kind of dynamic."

"A toxic family?" I question, my brows lowering.

Lennon looks forward, her eyes piercing in their intensity. "A fucking relationship, Noah. You're not used to a relationship."

Her words are like shards of glass, piercing my heart and drawing up memories I'd long forgotten.

I'd believed Alexis had a point when she confronted me about the time I spent studying–working my way through college–writing a fucking dissertation. She'd claimed her emotional needs had gone unmet–that she didn't mean to cheat with Hayes. *It just happened.* I'd be an idiot to not admit that I had a part in our demise. I hadn't been involved enough.

And maybe now I'm too involved.

Maybe I'm not cut out for this at all.

"Well, you're really just fucking me for the benefits, right?"

Her face falls. "That's not–"

"You said it, Lennon. And even if it was because you were angry, or if you truly believe you were lying, there has to be some truth there." My tone goes cold, like I've lost myself in this mess. I've gotten too close to Lennon. There's not a soul that could hurt me the way that she could in this moment, and it fucking terrifies me.

"I didn't *mean* any of that."

"Then what did you mean, exactly? Because from where I'm standing, you're the one who asked me to make out with you on a whim. It's not a far jump to believe that this was all just some sort of game to you." My fists clench. "You're letting your own insecurities justify how you treat others."

"I—" Lennon stands, taking a step closer. "That's not true."

"No, don't worry. I feel very enlightened."

"What do you feel enlightened about, Noah?" She folds her arms across her chest, watching me like she's already won.

The problem with that is I know exactly where it'll hurt the worst—the reason we are in this mess to begin with. And at this point, I'm too hurt and confused to stop myself. "You're not doing anything to prove them wrong right now." She jolts like I've hit her, but I don't stop. "Just because you hate yourself doesn't mean you get to demolish me in the process. The fact that I would defend you because I care about you, and the first place you go is to fucking admit that I'm just there to serve a purpose in your little bed-and-breakfast project." My tone bites, the words almost drawing blood by the way her face drains of color. "I was angry for you. That guy is a raging asshole, but I guess the apple didn't fall too far from the tree, now did it?"

Lennon clears her throat, and my jaw ticks from the way I'm grinding my teeth together—holding back the last thing in my mind—the barb that could unravel this whole thing altogether.

"By all means," she says, "go on. I assume you think I'm selfish and impulsive, too."

"Yeah," I say. "Yeah, I do think that. Because you are, Lennon. You absolutely fucking are."

I don't look back when I leave the room—the house. It isn't until the sky is dark that I return with Lennon long gone, nowhere to be found. I'm no sure where she went, nor do I take time to think about it.

Without a word, I collect my bags, drive to the nearest hotel, and drop a few hundred bucks for the night before changing my flight to the early morning.

What they say about Lennon might be correct, but as I turn off my phone and fly back to Ohio, I start to think what they say about me is just as true.

I'm not cut out for relationships at all.

Thirty

Lennon

The gurgling of the coffee pot echoes through the darkened kitchen, the clock reading five a.m. Despite the quiet, my mind continues to be so fucking loud.

Leaving to collect my thoughts earlier, walking around the neighborhood like a petulant teenager happened to be the wrong choice. Especially when I'd gotten back to the house to find that Noah had taken his bags and left.

The pain cut deeply, a wound that simply wouldn't stop bleeding no matter how much I tossed and turned.

Finally giving up to go to the kitchen, I'd never been more thankful to be a part of a family that sleeps in every chance they get. Which might be the only thing about my family I'm thankful for.

I can't blame them completely, though.

Somehow, I knew the rumors surrounding Noah hurt him. It's not like he hadn't told me what he *wanted* when Alexis cheated on him. He's been told repeatedly that he's no good at relationships, and this surface-level attraction is all that he could be worthy of. And even then, I exploited that weakness in a careless reaction to my father's cruelty.

I went for the jugular.

Noah was just the collateral damage.

The machine beeps, and I pad over to the refrigerator. Opening the door, I pull out the toffee nut creamer, find an appropriately fall-themed mug, and craft the saddest cup of coffee I've ever had the privilege of drinking.

I sit by the kitchen island to enjoy it.

"I told him off."

I spin on the stool, my sister standing in the entryway. The braid hanging over one shoulder looks less put together than the image of my sister that usually lingers somewhere in my memories. Her glasses sit high on her nose, eyes tired as she shifts to lean against the wall.

"Who?" I ask though I think I already know. I bring the steaming cup of coffee to my lips and sip the sugary concoction slowly. The mug provides a barrier of sorts—some distance to protect what's left of my dignity.

"Dad." Lorelei pushes off the wall, striding toward the cabinet to procure a mug. Less festive and woefully bitter as she neglects cream, sugar, and all that might make her hot bean water taste anything but burnt and disgusting.

"You're welcome for the coffee." I wince, the words sounding as bitter as her drink.

"Don't change the subject." Lorelei inhales deeply, gripping the hot mug in her hand.

I expected my sister to wear some silky matching pajama set. It's not that I didn't live with her growing up, but as she's matured to adulthood, her presence has become more and more absent. The ten-year age gap felt like a chasm between us, keeping a vast distance between who she is and the image I've crafted of her in my head. It's strange to see her sipping coffee in an oversized t-shirt and leggings. The holes in the shirt really sell the whole thing.

I wince again. "I wasn't trying to change the–"

"Yes." She cuts me off. "Yes, Lennon. You were. You've never been very good at heart-to-hearts, so I get it. Our family is not the most welcoming place for hopes and dreams and emotions and shit. But you were absolutely changing the subject."

I clear my throat, taking another sip, if only to distract from the uncomfortable sloshing in my stomach. Lorelei has never spoken to me like this. Our relationship is friendly but cold–surface level. It feels like a professional relationship you keep with someone you barely know at the office. It's not this.

"What did you say?" I ask, my voice low.

The clock from the dining room ticks in the distance, filling the space between our words.

Lorelei's brows furrow. "Not as much as I should have, but I've never been great at speaking up." A soft smile unfolds at the corner of her mouth when she glances sideways at me. "I'm really proud of you, Lennon."

Her words take me by surprise, my throat clogging with emotions I don't dare release. "For what," I joke, doing my best to feign casual indifference.

"For doing exactly what you fucking want." Lorelei takes a sip of coffee before setting the mug on the island with a soft sound. "You don't let his shit get to you. Instead of folding, you just keep moving in the direction you want to go." She shakes her head, staring at the liquid in her cup. "It's like no matter what, you refuse to cave to expectations. You wanted to go to college in Ohio. You did. You wanted a business degree, and you got it. You wanted a bed-and-breakfast, and now look at you." She waves a hand in my direction, and when her eyes finally turn on me, tears sting the corner of mine. I hate myself for it.

Lorelei takes another sip of coffee before tapping a finger on the shiny marble surface of the counter. The spotless surface hides anything that occurred in this very space less then a day ago. "I was honestly surprised when you asked me about the pediatric position," she continues. "You never seemed like you needed help with anything. You had it all figured out."

I scoff, shifting on the hard stool. "That's not how any of that felt. Besides, I had a lot to measure up to."

There's a brief pause, a moment for me to mull over the words she's spoken. They feel like a confession–a long overdue conversation we didn't know we needed.

My entire adult life has felt unstable. Sure, there are things I've wanted, but I've had to keep moving. If I stopped pursuing my goals, I was afraid there'd be no soft place to land–only the confirmation of my inadequacy and my destined failure.

Lorelei sighs. "I didn't want to be a fucking doctor."

My eyes widen, head snapping in her direction. "What?"

She laughs, but it sounds hollow. "A doctor. I didn't want to be a doctor at all. I had no idea what I wanted, but a gap year wasn't an option. Dad promised he wouldn't help if I took it. Something about making my own money for a year, meaning I could do it for myself." She looks at me, vulnerability shining in her gaze. "Obviously, that's ridiculous. I don't know. I picked something that sounded good; got so far into it I couldn't back out. By the time I was in med school, I'd acquired so much debt that any other job didn't make sense."

I think about the disconnect I'd felt during Lorelei's time in med school. I'd been attending high school, high on resentment and spite and barrelling toward a dream I truly wanted but wasn't supported in having.

Lorelei hardly talked to me, visiting for short stints and spending them holed up in her room studying. Dad praised her work ethic–her drive. I suppose his words helped form my opinions about what was happening around me. His ideas always held far too much weight, anyway.

Plus, it's not like I talked to Lorelei. I didn't want to pine for some kind of sibling relationship that didn't exist–didn't want to fall into the typical younger sibling role begging for attention.

I chew on my lip, eyes fixed to my cup. "You seemed so motivated, though."

"Ahh," she says. "That good old external pressure pushing me toward something I didn't even want. I think Devon is the only good thing I got out of it all." Her fist rests on her cheek as she looks at me, her green eyes a mirror of my own. "Don't worry, I ripped him a new asshole for that comment he made at dinner."

I chuckle, easing some of the tension before saying the one thing on my mind. "I guess I didn't realize all of that." I clear my throat, trying to force the tears away. "Probably pretty selfish of me not to notice."

Lorelei nudges me with her shoulder. "Sure," she says. "But everyone is selfish. It's kind of hard not to be when you're always fucking there, you know?" She waves a hand around. "Your thoughts. They're your closest companion."

I nod, hating the way my stomach churns. Noah's words echo in my mind.

Yeah, I do think that. Because you are, Lennon. You absolutely fucking are.

"Hey," she says, nudging me again. "Remember last Christmas when mom was about to die of dysentery because of that undercooked chicken."

I chuckle. "Yeah."

"I wasn't the one cleaning that shit up and running all over town for some meds."

I wince, the scent of vomit lingering in my nose. "You know Bailey kept trying to eat the puke."

"That dog was both blind and deaf. I'm sure she didn't know what she was eating." Lorelei takes another sip of coffee. "I felt bad last April when Mom had to put her down, but I couldn't do another year of letting her out all hours of the night."

I laugh now—the sound more relaxed. "That was terrible, wasn't it?"

Her laugh mixes with mine. "The worst."

There's another pause, one filled with all the confessions of the last twenty minutes.

"I mean it, though, Lennon." Lorelei stands up, placing her empty coffee mug in the sink before turning around to face me. The cup sits there, unrinsed—the one item making our cold house a little more lived in. "Dad has been really good at loving us in the highlights, but he struggles with everything else." She leans against the counter, folding her arms. "Maybe one day he'll go to therapy and get over it, but I promise you, you're doing a lot of really cool shit—and Noah defending you." She whistles. "Hot. Not even going to lie."

I look down, hating the way his name draws guilt from the deepest parts of my chest. "Yeah, well," I start. "I'm not sure if Noah and I will pan out in the end."

She cocks her head to one side. "Why do you say that?"

"He left."

"That doesn't mean anything."

My brows furrow. "It kind of says a lot about the current climate of the very new, very fragile relationship." I draw my mug to my lips.

"I think it just says you both need to apologize and fuck it out."

I choke, coughing as the coffee threatens to come out of my nose.

Lorelei smiles, pushing off the counter. "Maybe he'll paint some more cabinets for you, too."

She winks, striding out of the kitchen and leaving me with my thoughts.

Thirty-One

Noah

I bring the beer bottle to my lips, gulping down the amber liquid in an attempt to wash away whatever shit I said to Lennon.

The stinging at the back of my throat feels like retribution. It's also keeping me from continuing to spew emotional shit at Ryan, something he doesn't deserve.

Noises from the bar echo across the polished concrete floors. Games sound along with cheering, drowning out the steady thump in my chest—the pained beating of my heart.

"I didn't realize you were engaged." Ryan grips his own beer bottle, swirling it between his thumb and finger while staring at the wooden table, our usual bar spot.

I set my drink down harder than I originally planned and wince. "Yeah, well. It didn't seem important. Five years ago is a long time."

Ryan's dark eyes cut to mine, clearly seeing through my charade. "You almost married the woman. That's a lifetime of commitment engulfed in fire. Also, you're allowed to be hurt, you idiot. It doesn't make you more of a man to act like shit doesn't bother you."

"Hm." I take another sip, avoiding his gaze.

"Speaking of that, what about Lennon?"

My stomach drops, and the entire room feels heavy. "What about her?"

"You said dinner was terrible, you knew you shouldn't have gotten into a relationship, to begin with, and you also referred to the entire holiday as a massive shit show that ended exactly as you expected."

He waits for me to respond, but I don't.

Ryan runs a hand down his face in frustration, the new tattoo on his hand standing out more than the others. "So," he starts. "What actually happened?"

I take another drink of beer, knowing I should slow down, but something about the bite of it helps. The bubbles burn, and that distracts from the burning in my chest.

Ryan presses, and I cave, rehashing the whole thing in what is probably too much detail.

"Anyway," I continue, nearing the end of my long venting session. "I walked the fuck out. If she doesn't think I'm equipped to be in a relationship, then I might as well not be in one. It's served me just fine for the past five years. I've had no complaints."

"You're hurt," Ryan says, and I scowl.

"I mean–" There's no sense in lying. "Sure, yeah." I look away, briefly sucking on my teeth. "Whatever."

We sit in silence, and I can feel his gaze on my face, analyzing the situation in a way that makes me uncomfortable. It spurs me on into speaking more bullshit.

"You know," I start, leaning forward and gripping my beer by the neck of the bottle. "One thing goes wrong, and she just implodes. Like a fucking bomb. She attacks everyone with little regard for them. You should hear the way she spoke to her father–how cold she got."

"Yeah, dude," he says, so calm in the wake of my heightened emotions. "She hurt you, so of course you're pissed. What was it you said to her at the end? I didn't get the full scope of that. Something about her father being a raging asshole."

Guilt slams into me unwelcomed. I look down at the table. He knows he's got me. "I told her she was just like him." The confession burns more than anything thus far. "I told her she hated herself."

Ryan sits back, staring at me, and it's as if I can feel everything he's thinking from where he sits.

His judgment drowns out the sounds of the bar, narrowing my focus on whatever advice he has to offer. I suppose that was the point of this meeting–to seek advice. Or maybe it was to hang out. I honestly can't remember.

When he finally says something, it takes me by surprise. "You've spent this entire hangout being an insufferable sulking asshole who can't stop talking about Thanksgiving. I'm actually kind of sick of it." Ryan places his elbows on the table. "I did an awesome fucking back piece at the tattoo shop, and I was going to show that shit to you. You're ruining this entire hangout."

I scoff. "Yeah, thanks."

"Noah, it might be insensitive of me, but you have to get your shit together. Okay, she shouldn't have taken it out on you, but her family insulted her for an entire dinner. You escalated the situation trying to be noble, and then when she lashed out, you made it about you."

My face falls, the color draining completely.

Yeah, I do think that. Because you are, Lennon. You absolutely fucking are.

"She–" I don't know what I'm saying, but it doesn't matter because he cuts me off.

"Reacted? Yeah, that usually happens in tense situations. People are wired for self-preservation, you asshat. She probably grew up with one mechanism to protect herself, and you pulled that rug out from under her. She was selfish, sure, but so were you."

I lean back in my chair, looking at the bright lights of the bar hanging overhead. The industrial ceiling scratches over the entire place. "It's whatever, now," I mumble. "She hates me."

"Does she?" Ryan raises a brow. "It seems like she cares just as much about you as you do her. You both knew the exact thing that would hurt the most. How do you suppose you guys knew that?" He takes another drink of beer before continuing. "I know exactly what to say to Wyatt to hurt him because I pay attention–because I know him."

"Okay," I say, blinking.

"To be loved is to be known."

That word–*love*–has me bouncing my knee beneath the table. I've thought about it–I've thought about it a lot, actually. And while I don't know if we've been together long enough for that to be the case, I *do* know what direction things are going–*were* going.

I wouldn't have asked for a relationship if I thought myself incapable of loving her.

Pulling out my phone, I draw up her contact, staring at the last string of messages we sent in Minneapolis. Sometime between last week and this weekend, I've memorized every word and hilarious gif–unable to conjure up anything to say, but now I think I have something. It might be hopeless, but it's worth a shot.

She doesn't respond, and I second-guess the entire thing. I should have apologized now. I should have sent paragraphs about how I fucked up, how I said the worst thing I could think of.

When the three dots pop up, hope sparks in my chest.

Lennon: I need to hang some shelving in the kitchen, too. Tomorrow at nine?

Noah: I'll be there.

Thirty-Two

Lennon

The thought of Noah coming over makes my stomach churn. I said a lot of shit in Minneapolis, and we haven't talked in over a week.

There's a very real fear that he's coming over to continue telling me all the ways I'm a terrible person. I would most likely deserve it.

Luckily, Griffin had a last-minute gig in Nashville, so when Ellis called me yesterday, I first made fun of her for wallowing, and then invited her over. We spent the entire evening talking about everything but Noah—rehashing old memories from college.

I wash another plate, setting it in the drying rack before picking up a bowl when Ellis comes down from the upstairs.

"That new bed is immaculate. I could sleep in it forever. You've truly outdone yourself on the furniture."

I smile, squeezing the sponge to make suds appear. "You're the first person to stay in my bed-and-breakfast, Ellis. The compliment means a lot, but it's actually just a memory foam mattress topper I got on sale."

She leans over the counter next to me, her hair wild and matching pj set somewhat askew. "I must get one."

I laugh, continuing washing the dishes from our all night snacking session while the morning sunlight bathes the kitchen in a soft glow.

"So," she starts, turning until her back is leaning against the counter next to me.

"So," I mock.

"Are we going to talk about Noah?"

I've never been a particularly anxious person, but her words spur me closer to the edge. Briefly, I consider taking edibles to soothe my rapidly beating heart. "No," I say. "But he will be here in two hours. You're welcome to stay."

She chuckles. "Not after that bonfire. I'm not staying here at all."

I wince, grabbing a towel and drying the plate I washed earlier. "Actually, we are kind of in a weird place right now."

Ellis's brows furrow. "What do you mean?" She must see something on my face because she has the mind to get in it. "What do you actually mean?"

"Some things happened with my family."

"Your mom?"

"No."

Ellis's face falls, and I give in. The version is somewhat abridged. I don't want to divulge too many details–weigh her down with all of my shit when she's supposed to be here because she was feeling lonely.

"Well," she starts. "I've never seen you truly *all in* with a relationship before. You usually keep some distance. Showing Noah your dad's glowing personality seems like maybe we have some deep feelings here?"

I don't answer and just keep drying the dishes, but the longer the silence stretches on, the more uncomfortable I get. Ellis expects an answer, and I feel obligated to give one.

"I've spent a lot of time trying to prove my father wrong–" I wave my hands around. "About all of this."

Ellis smiles, something akin to the Cheshire cat. It's like she knows something I don't. "It's so funny how you walk around seeking approval while pretending that isn't what you're doing."

I glare at her. "You're a real bitch, you know?"

"And so are you. It's why we are friends." Her smile eventually falls, and I turn to face her, noting the seriousness in her gaze. "Listen, you were there for me last spring when my dad showed up."

"May that fucker rest in absolute distress. Burn in the lake of fire for all eternity."

She huffs a laugh. "Don't distract. You were there last year, and I want you to know that I'm here right now if you need to talk."

My brows lower. "I think I need a distraction before he comes over."

"Okay." She pauses, thinking of what to say. "Griffin is acting really weird about my birthday this year. He's been all off, and it's making me nervous."

I smile, looking out the window that showcases the backyard, now muddy and brown. I wish it would snow already. "Yeah," I say. "I wouldn't worry. I'm pretty sure Griffin just acts strange because he's in love with you."

"And Noah?" she asks, drawing my attention back to her.

I'm silent, and I think it says a lot.

When I started this thing, I knew I needed to be careful of my heart, but somehow I lost myself on the way. It's not that Noah's *words* hurt the most. They did hurt, absolutely. But it was the fact that he was the one to say them that cut the deepest.

I hadn't thought about what that meant—what it indicated, but I think Ellis might be right. I might not love him, but I care. I care so fucking much, and it's scary as shit.

I might love him.

It wouldn't take much for me to cross that line.

I clear my throat, fully ready to deflect. "So," I start. "I need to reorganize the hutch I thrifted in the dining room. I have some mismatched teacups that need to go in there. Want to help?"

Ellis doesn't press. She just rolls her eyes. "Sure, Lennon. Sure."

Thirty-Three

Noah

I let myself into the house.

Somehow, I can't find it in me to feel bad about it, especially when I notice Lennon leaned over the kitchen counter, scrubbing the grout on the backsplash like it's her personal enemy.

I stand there, watching as my emotions war within me. I've never been more scared of the woman, and we've come a long way since those first days of her hating my guts–or something. Maybe she never really hated me to begin with.

In an effort to separate myself from being a creepier version of Edward Cullen, I clear my throat, announcing my presence and causing her to spin.

"I'm supposed to be doing that," I say, and her face falls, the rag still grasped in her hand like she's trying to strangle it.

"You're late."

I put my hands in the pockets of my slacks. "My car pep talk took a bit longer than I anticipated." I wince.

The elaborate speech I'd planned out, first my head, and then my notes app, seems like a terrible idea. I don't think I'll remember all the most important points, and reading it from my phone seems like it would make me a real tool.

"Why did you need a pep talk?" she asks, frozen in place.

Well, here it goes.

"I needed to gas myself up to tell you that I'm sorry."

"Don't–"

I hold up a hand. "I have to. I tried to hurt you. I knew exactly what I was saying as I was saying it. It was hard not to react to what you said, Lennon, because I want a relationship with you so fucking badly. It's the first time I've tried to pursue anything after Alexis, and I want it with *you*. God, do I fucking want it."

She blinks, and I swear her green eyes take on a glassy sheen–lined with tears that refuse to fall. It makes them look brighter in the morning light. "You said want."

I almost don't hear her, pressing on. "And it was selfish of me to make it about me. I wanted to be noble, to be a good partner to you. I wanted you to feel like I had your back, and I guess I fucked that up. But I didn't mean to–" her words finally register, derailing my train of thought. "What?" I ask.

"You said want. You said that you *want* a relationship."

My brow furrows. "Yeah, I–"

"Not wanted," she adds, and I catch her meaning.

I clear my throat, my gaze meeting hers across the room. "Of course, I still want you." I blink. "You aren't your reactions to the people who hurt you. That's clearly something I need to work on, too."

Her gaze flicks to the ground. "I'm sorry I let you take all of my anger. I wasn't really mad at you, I just didn't–"

I take a step forward, then another–moving until I'm standing directly in front of her. When her eyes meet mine, they thaw something in me–softening all the icy parts of myself until there's nothing left but warmth.

And her.

My hand rises to her cheek, and thank fuck she doesn't pull away. "I don't want this to be over," I say, my heart pounding a steady rhythm in my chest. "For one, the house is still a fucking mess. You need my help."

She laughs, closing her eyes and leaning into my touch. It warms me even more. "I started on the grout."

I lean forward, my lips hovering over hers. "And you're doing a terrible fucking job," I whisper as she steps closer.

"I'm glad you're here, Noah."

I'd spent a lot of time thinking about what Ryan said–the advice he'd given me when I forced him into listening to my sob story.

For the longest time, I'd denied myself what I wanted–believing myself unworthy–settling.

I don't want to settle anymore.

My lips brush against hers–a promise of a kiss. "I wouldn't want to be anywhere else." I do it again, tasting late autumn air–like cinnamon and coffee. "I'm sorry," I repeat, hoping she hears how much I fucking mean it. "I don't want to be without you, Lennon."

She breathes me in before pressing her mouth to mine. The kiss is soft–charged with all the emotion of the past week. When she finally pulls back, her eyes are open, staring at me in a way that makes my skin heat.

"I don't want to be without you, either," she whispers. "Do you want to watch a movie?" she asks.

I smile, my hand still resting on the side of her face as my thumb strokes softly. "Sure, Lennon." My smile widens. "I'd love to watch a movie with you. Especially if it's one nobody has seen before."

Epilogue

Lennon

Friends and family fill the house as I find my way onto the front porch, a hard seltzer gripped in one hand.

The porch holds sturdy, and the interior consists of mismatched decor, but for some reason, it all works. While I thrifted most things, the bookshelves Noah and I purchased still stand in the living room, a reminder of all the hard work we put into this place.

It's hard to believe I've made it this far—a grand opening.

Something warms in my chest knowing all these people showed up for *me*. And tomorrow night, we host our first guests.

"It looks good," Ellis says from her spot near the porch railing. Cass beams at me, her blonde hair falling in natural waves over her shoulders, sunglasses atop her head.

Last April, she had decided against finding a new house, and opted to move on a farm forty minutes away. I guess the job included a house at the end of the drive–part of the compensation for running the farm.

I didn't know she knew anything about horses, but I guess I was wrong. Apparently, she grew up riding.

The job's changed her, that's for sure. Her skin is sun-kissed, and she hasn't brought up her ex in a while.

It's good for her–I think.

"Yeah, yeah," I say, waving off Ellis's compliment. "Unimportant. Let's see it, bitch."

Ellis rolls her eyes, but the gentle smile on her lips gives her away. "Old news," she groans.

I hold my hand out, waiting. "I don't care. Show me again."

She grabs my hand. A solitaire diamond decorates her finger, carefully held by the twisting rose gold band. The ring looks like it was forged by an elf or something. It's perfect for her.

I have to give it to Griffin–the rock is huge.

A warm arm wraps around my waist, Noah's expensive cologne invading my nostrils. He smells like home. "Don't go swimming with that thing," he says, staring at Ellis's ring.

We were somehow able to keep the secret.

A true show of my devotion to my friend. I wanted her to have the full experience, and damn did she.

Ellis chuckles before taking a sip of her drink. "It's not that crazy."

Cass nudges her. "Don't lie to us."

"Okay, it's fucking huge," Ellis admits.

The group breaks into laughter, and Noah kisses my temple, warmth radiating from his touch. His lips brush my ear before he whispers, "I'm proud of you, you know."

I feel stupid, but my entire soul is glowing at his praise. Things may still be rocky with my dad, but there's little I can do about that. The good news is I feel closer to Lorelei than I ever have. She and Mom plan on coming to the Inn later this week to check it out.

"Yeah," I say. "I know."

Noah pulls back, that dimple popping in his cheek. "I'm going to go find Griffin."

When he leaves, Ellis's expression changes, her dark hair swirling with the gentle summer breeze. "So," she starts. "Your dad still won't see the place."

I scoff. "No, but the rest of the family is coming next week."

Ellis chuckles. "Just don't get caught fucking in the barn."

I roll my eyes, glancing at Cass and noticing the way her cheeks tinge pink.

"Speaking of barns," I say. "How's the new job?"

She clears her throat. "It's good!" Cass tucks a strand of hair behind her ear. "I can actually carry the water buckets now without wanting to die."

I chuckle in response.

"I think you should arm wrestle Griffin," Ellis adds. "Assert your dominance just in case he ever steps out of line."

Cass lets out a soft laugh. "That seems like Lennon's job."

When I turn, I notice an old pickup rumble down the gravel road—one I've never seen before. A man steps out, cowboy hat firmly placed atop his head, sun-kissed skin, and a pair of snug Levi's Noah wouldn't be caught dead in.

"Um," Ellis starts as we all stare. He seems upset, stomping his boots on the rocks as he makes his way to the porch. "Who is that?"

Cass's face goes white—like a ghost, and I can't help the way I step protectively in front of her.

"Well," she says, her voice small. "So," she starts again. "That's actually my boss."

Acknowledgements

Please pretend I wrote a phenomenal introduction to the acknowledgments of this book. I'd like to imagine it was poetic, thought-provoking, witty, and enjoyable. Whatever that looks like for you, you can insert that here.

There is a team of fierce supporters behind every book I've written, and this book is no different.

Livy Hart, my bestie, my sounding board, my personal romance land Suriel, thank you for your support, undying love, and devotion. Because of you, this book is not only the spiciest book I've ever written, but it is complete. You sacrificed your time and energy to listen to no less than five thousand hours of voice memos. With sore muscles and sweat-slicked skin, you worked in the trenches to read this manuscript, combing through every word to ensure that Noah's ass got the appropriate amount of airtime. Thrusts became plentiful, dirty talk became abundant. You carried this novel, inspired my love of romance with your own writing, and allowed me to be completely delusional when necessary. I'm forever grateful for you and your encouragement. I don't know what I did to deserve you, and Sebastain, your hottest brainchild.

Thank you to Wednesday for being generally encouraging whether you like the book or not. I know you prefer fantasy novels and reading any of this caused you true physical pain. I appreciate your friendship.

Thank you to Kenna, my friend and editor, without you, none of my books would be good. I know what you're thinking as you read this, and stop. Seriously, stop. Did you see the extra comma? I left it there for you as a reminder of all you do.

Reanna, thank you for proofreading my books and combing through them for all of the extra errors I introduce while panicking and changing small things last minute. You make the public believe I'm intelligent.

Thank you to my husband for listening to me yap about my story ideas.

I'd like to thank my sister-in-law, Sarah. For starters, thank you for going to the haunted prison with me. That was the scariest shit I've ever been through, and I'm certain I nearly had a medical event. Also, thank you for listening to me yap about this story on the way back from that frightening and fun activity. You're the best.

Kristin, Kera, and Kayla, thank you for making Books Gowns and Crowns Chapter 3 so much fun. And thank you for listening to me yap about this book (I'm realizing I yap a lot).

Thank you, Nicole for your kindness, support, and willingness to read my work.

Finally, thank you to my readers. I will never understand why you consider showing up for me, but I'm forever grateful.